THE POLICE ARE CONVINCED HIGH SCHOOL SENIOR JOHN BATEMAN VICIOUSLY MURDERED THREE FRIENDS WHILE HUNTING DEER.

The sheriff's office thinks Bateman, a model high school senior and son of a prominent citizen, brutally murdered his three companions on a south Alabama whitetail deer hunt. They don't buy the tale he tells of a huge buck that somehow managed to kill all three of the armed men. They are a hair's breath away from indicting him for murder when evidence begins to surface suggesting that something strange and seriously wrong happened out there in the woods. Could it be that John's unbelievable story is actually true? John must risk his own life in the final showdown to prove his innocence beyond a doubt.

"Sandy Harris shows his love of the Southern outdoors and a good mystery in *At First Light*. You'll smell the scent of pine, and blood, in his prose." — *Johnny D. Boggs, author of Killstraight and Whiskey Kills.*

i

"Sandy Harris has taken an unusual premise, mixed in strong, memorable characters and several surprises in this strong debut mystery. Highly recommended!" — *Gordon Aalborg ... author of The Specialist and Dining With Devils ... and — coming in 2018 — River of Porcupines.*

"It's always enjoyable to discover a new author who has crafted a unique, suspenseful tale. I look forward to seeing what Sandy Harris does next. He's one to watch." — *Ben Rehder, Edgar and Shamus Award finalist.*

"In *At First Light*, a story where one hunter's bad deeds turn deadly, author Sandy Harris's passion and great respect for wildlife shines through. A great read!" — *Kimberli A. Bindschatel, award winning author of the Poppy McVie, Saving Animals One Book at a Time series.*

"In this interesting first novel, Sandy Harris employs the gritty prose and character development of the 'detective' genre to turn out a taut hunting story in which the hunters become the hunted. His Moby Dick with antlers will keep visitors to the woods looking over their shoulders long after they've finished the book." — *E. Donnall Thomas Jr., author of Whitefish Can't Jump and The Language of Wings.*

AT FIRST LIGHT

Sandy Harris

Moonshine Cove Publishing, LLC
Abbeville, South Carolina U.S.A.

ISBN: 978-1-945181-122
Library of Congress PCN: 2017906041
Copyright 2017 by Sandy Harris

Front cover painting by Stephanie Burdick Harrison; cover and interior design by Moonshine Cove staff.

For Dennis, who told me about the drunk geese.

ABOUT THE AUTHOR

Sandy Harris grew up on a farm in eastern North Carolina.  There, with grit under his fingernails and dirt in his shoes, he learned to love the land and the critters that call it home. After receiving degrees in Wildlife Biology from NC State, and Forest Biology from Auburn University, he has spent time as a farmer, Sunday School teacher, biologist, forester, environmental scientist, and freelance writer, chronicling his hunting adventures with primitive bows he carves from trees. Influenced early on by Mickey Spillane's *Mike Hammer* TV series, he's always had a soft spot in his heart for a good mystery. In *At First Light*, his first published novel, he cleverly intertwines his love for the natural world with those classic, gritty crime mysteries. Sandy resides in Wetumpka, AL with his wife, Kristy, and two sons, Ethan and Eli, and is currently working on his second book.

I kept my bow half-drawn, a shaft
Set straight across the velvet haft.
Alert and vigilant I stood,
Scanning the lake, the sky, the wood.

— *The Witchery of Archery*
Maurice Thompson, 1878.

AT FIRST

LIGHT

Part I

Chapter 1

John Bateman sat quietly at the plain steel table, fingers laced together in his lap, thumbs twiddling. Front to back and side to side, the nicotine stained walls of the little interrogation room seemed to tighten around him each time he exhaled, like a massive constrictor slowly squeezing the life out of its prey. When he could feel something besides the mental phenomenon of claustrophobia, his body reminded him of the physical torture he'd endured. The deep scratches on his arms stung, his legs ached, his back screamed, his mind, or what was left of it, begged for several hours of good sleep. There was no doubt that yesterday and the day before were the two worst days of his short seventeen years . . . but at least he was alive.

While John's thumbs made those compact little circles, he imagined the large and frantic circles his legs and feet must have made trying to escape. He closed his eyes, and he was there again, a frightened kid running for his life. A half-mile through the woods, a mile and a half on the county road, and somehow he was still running flat out when he reached the state highway. The sprint slowed to a labored jog, then a fast walk; his body was at its limit, as fires ignited in his quads and calves. Tired legs soon cramped, and there he was, limping along the black-top, begging God with every step to either bring help or to make the end painless and quick.

The highway markers said he was on his fifth mile when he heard a rumble on the road behind him. A bolt of electricity careened down his spine, and he quickly turned, hoping that his legs would work again. When it topped the rise, the approaching truck's chrome grill glimmered a triumphant metallic grin and he exhaled a long breath of relief. The prayer had been answered.

***

He'd walked through the doors of the Sheriff's office just after lunch, and that's when the rest of the nightmare began. The afternoon and evening with his new law enforcement friends were interminable, the long night even worse, and when the sun finally peeked in the holding cell's small window, he was still sitting on the edge of the cot in the same position they left him when the deputy called for 'lights out.' A new day had dawned, but John somehow knew it was going to be more of the same. Twice he went back through it all, just as he remembered, just as it happened, but the county investigator wasn't buying it. Captain Meyers yelled, screamed, threatened, stomped, and cursed — almost everything he could get away with, yet John somehow endured. Now, the shaken teen was waiting for Meyers to start in on him again, but he knew that short of physical violence, it couldn't get any worse than last time. Hurricane Meyers had made landfall there in that little interrogation room, a Category 5 super storm, but so far he hadn't laid a finger on him. At least not yet.

While the Captain reviewed his notes, John squirmed nervously in the unnatural silence. He began to sense that the irritation he felt was not accidental. The room was noticeably warmer than the rest of the building, the chair he sat in teetered diagonally at the slightest shift of weight, the table seemed to be a few inches shorter than it should be, and the ceiling was far less than the standard eight feet. Everything about that little room was designed to make life irritating, but it was the silence that was doing the most damage. John, desperately trying to make something out of nothing, consciously began to listen for something besides the air moving though his own nose. No phones rang, no typewriter's keys clicked, there was no idle chatter from the deputies down the hall, no sounds of any kind seeped in from the world beyond those dingy walls. The quiet seemed to be alive, a being that might be found in every principal's office or library, leering dolefully over those who even thought about speaking. Oddly, John could feel his own thoughts slowly being erased. Perhaps they, too, were offending the silence?

The seams that held him together were starting to fray, and his fragmented brain responded the only way it could — groping for anything familiar — trying to retain some semblance of order or normality. Then he heard it.

Tick... tick... tick... tick... tick...

The Timex on Meyers' wrist cheerfully ticked the seconds away, same as it did every minute of every day, no matter who lived or died. Noticing those little sounds in the stark quiet, John felt a sliver of calm. Finally he had found something that hadn't changed. Time.

The momentary relief was short lived though, as the hopeless desire for everything else to be as it was completely enveloped him like a tight-fitting straight jacket. *How could anyone go on living a normal life after seeing what I saw?* He didn't know how to answer that simple question, but was certain that reality was forcing him to acknowledge that no matter how hard he tried to forget, things were never going to be the same. But somehow, someway, those orderly, predictable, normal ticks strangely, almost eerily, began to sooth his worries. Clearing his mind, he listened and began to count. He reached sixty once, then twice, and then counted fifty-two more ticks in the dead stillness before Meyers adjusted his seat and loudly sighed, breaking his concentration. When his diaphragm hit bottom, Meyers casually flicked his wrist and the pad was airborne. John, still focused on the watch, didn't see it coming. The heavy pad landed on his side of the table with a loud *bang*, startling him into a full body flinch. When the kid looked up, he expected to see blood running down his shirt and Captain Meyers gripping a smoking gun.

Meyers' starched white button-down shirt almost creaked as he leaned forward; the end of the Marlboro cigarette glowed red and hissed lightly, while a bead of sweat trickled down the bridge of his crooked nose. "John," the Captain's voice quivered a little, forcing back a laugh, "are you sure this is the story you want to stick with?"

John didn't answer, didn't even nod his head.

"You realize what you are saying, right? This report can be permanent. If you make me type it up this way and it becomes official, you're finished. You hear me? You can kiss the rest of your senior year and college goodbye. They'll write you up a one way ticket to the nut house and haul you outta here in a custom fit straight jacket. You hear me? You'll be done. *Finished.* You can bet your bottom dollar on it John."

Silence.

Meyers' face began to turn red. He stopped for a moment to compose himself, took a deep breath, then very slowly and deliberately reached out and tapped the tip of his index finger in the center of the notebook three times, "You look at those pages and tell me with a straight face you believe it. Tell me you believe what I wrote down there — your words, John. Your words!"

The Captain reached into his briefcase sitting on the floor beside his chair. He palmed six pictures — two each of Albert Rutledge, Renfro Abernathy, and Kirby McNeil — and spread them across the table. Each body was situated on a stainless steel examination table, covered from the waist down by a white sheet. John saw the neat, perfectly round little holes in their chests and bellies, and the massive amounts of dark blue and black skin discoloration. Between bruises, the skin was the color of death — a dull, chalky shade of gray. Renn's jaw was misshapen several inches below his right ear, probably broken from the impact. Clearly the photographs had been taken by the Medical Examiner in Montgomery. They were not distasteful or excessively gruesome. In fact, they could have been stock photos from any medical school textbook. The bodies, however, were not some random cadavers, they were John's friends, and friends of his father. The teen's emotions rushed back as he stifled a groan and quickly looked away.

Meyers opened a manila folder and started thumbing through a new stack of papers, "Preliminary reports from the Medical Examiner say that the cause of death for each was from something called hypovolemia, but not before they experienced a tremendous amount of contusions and hematomas. Do you know what all that means?"

John shook his head. He knew that contusion was the medical term for bruising, and he had heard of the other two words, but wasn't sure what they meant.

"It's just fancy medical talk for they all bled to death while someone was beating the shit out of them."

Still John said nothing.

Meyers' face flushed again, and he brought down his hand hard on the table. The loud bang echoed across the small room, doubtless startling even the deputies watching behind the two way mirror in the observation room.

"Dammit John, this is no joke. You've got to give me something to work with here! Something that explains this." Meyers was nearly screaming. "Three people are dead. Do you see them there in the pictures? Friends you and I and your father have known for a long time. Hell, Al was the best man at your folk's wedding, and Kirby worked for your dad. They all knew you since you were knee high to a grasshopper.

"Al, Renn, Kirby — all of them died at *your* hunting camp while *you* were there." The Captain paused a long moment, then he casually gathered the pictures, shuffled through them a couple of times as if he'd never seen them before, then placed them and the medical report back into his briefcase. Meyers shook his head and leaned forward trying to catch something in the kid's body language he might have missed earlier. "Can't you see how this looks? Well, if you can't let me be the first to tell you, it ain't good! You've *got* to help me understand what went on down there."

Chapter 2

The kid wasn't talking. Frustrated, Captain Jonas Meyers, lead investigator and second in command of the Jessup County Sheriff's office, cursed under his breath, stood, swept his notebook and empty coffee cup off the table, and stormed out of the room. He stomped down the hallway, more for show than anything, but was walking normally by the time he reached his office. Meyers pushed open his door, placed the pad and cup on his cluttered desk, and collapsed into his chair, holding a throbbing head with both hands. A veteran of law enforcement for nearly twenty years, he'd heard some doozies before, but what he had just listened to was the best one yet. *A cigarette would make it better.* He knew it was a lie, but he had to do something. There was no way to attempt to wrap his mind around something like this without help . . . and a lot of it.

He stared at the stained cup through the cracks in his fingers. The faded words 12th PRECINCT ATLANTA PD baked into its worn finish seemed to be brighter and clearer than they had been in a long time. A smile crept onto his lips reminiscing about the Peachtree District — ahh, the good ole days. For some, downtown Atlanta is just a dirty, bustling, overpopulated nightmare. For a rookie cop, it was nirvana. Looking back on it now, he was certain that he'd suggest it to any neophyte lawman. A week walking the beat in any big city might equal ten, maybe even twenty years in a sleepy small town. There was always action just around the next corner, and when you are just starting out, action is what you needed.

The memories came flooding back, his first partner, his first paycheck, his first arrest, but the nostalgia was quickly quelled by a festering conversation just outside his window. The shades were drawn blocking his view, but the voice he heard seeping through the paper-thin walls was the unmistakable rattle of Mrs. Rhonda Avert. She was sternly arguing with her twin rug-rats about whether they deserved a candy bar from the drugstore, given their poor behavior at church yesterday morning. Apparently they had not, and when the gavel dropped on a less than favorable verdict the children began to wail loudly, irritating his already irritated brain.

Those are the breaks, kids . . . I suppose next Sunday you'll think twice before sailing paper airplanes into the baptistery during the Doxology. Now, Madam Avert, kindly remove those public nuisances from the street before I walk out there and arrest all three of you for disturbing my peace. Almost at request of his mental warning, and to his surprise, the ruckus faded away to nothing, and satisfied that the peace had once again been kept, the Captain began to move for the unopened pack of Marlboros in his shirt pocket. It was then he noticed the lanky figure standing at his door.

"Well, Jonas?" The deep, booming voice flooded the room followed by its owner. David Butters, the Sheriff of Jessup County, casually strode to the Captain's messy desk, found a clean spot near the edge, and leaned a bony hip.

"Well, what?" Meyers looked annoyed, still reaching for the cigarettes.

"You know what I meant. Did it get any better this time?"

"Depends on what you mean by better."

Butters sipped from his own cup, and absently twisted one end of his graying handlebar mustache. "Whoa there, cowboy, before you go and say something I can't get over. I know all this business has you on edge, but there's no need to be thick headed about it. And don't forget, until the voting citizens of this fine county deem otherwise, I'm still your boss. Now if you don't mind, let's try this again." The Sheriff deliberately cleared his throat as if he was about to start a campaign speech. "Did it get any better this time? Did he make any better sense of it?"

"No, not really." Meyers sighed. "He's sticking to it pretty close. If anything, he went into more detail than the time before." He slid the notebook forward. "Take a look at it yourself if you like. It's a bit messy, but I believe you can still follow it."

Meyers propped his elbows on the edge of the desk, and methodically rubbed both temples with his fingertips. He knew what he wanted to say, but now wasn't the time. David Butters was as straight-laced as they come, and a crude joke about it probably would not be received well. Something more appropriate quickly replaced the harsh thought. "Every square inch of this is pure lunacy, but you want to know what the craziest part of it is? I think he really believes it happened that way."

Sheriff Butters moved his hand from his mustache to the back of his neck. He grimaced slightly while working stiff muscles. "Well, just stick with it. He's a smart one, and smart ones are usually the toughest to break."

Meyers watched him carefully, dreading to hear the words he knew were coming. Over the years, he'd heard the sermon a thousand times. It was his *go to* statement whenever they had someone in the tank that wasn't cooperating. The Captain rolled his eyes as Butters took a deep breath and said, "We've got to make this kid realize that we know the yarn he's spinning is a lie. A complete fairy tale. No matter how conniving he's trying to be, or how off he is in the head, when he starts to realize we aren't buying it, eventually he'll start doubting it himself. When he starts to doubt, that's when he'll crack. It may take a while, but it'll happen . . . eventually."

The Sheriff ignored the chance to look at the Captain's notes, and took another sip of coffee. "I talked with his folks a little while ago. Clayton ain't happy about any of it, especially since it looks like they are going to be stuck in St. Louis at least another night, possibly two. I didn't tell him how bad it looks, but I assured him that no accusations or formal charges have been made, and we are treating him merely as a person of interest. And when or if it looks like that might change, we'd be sure to give him plenty of warning."

Butters chased down another sip and smacked his lips. "And Jonas, please remember what I said yesterday. We're just supposed to be asking questions, and he's supposed to be answering them to the best of his ability. No tricks, no games. I wasn't in the observation room for all of it, but when I was, you were getting mighty close to over-doing it. In fact, I was about two seconds from snatching you out of there one time. Hollerin' and screamin' ain't going to get it done right now. With a kid like this, we can't afford to be too aggressive. If you scare him bad enough, he might just quit on us . . . shut down completely. If he does that, we're finished here, and the next time we'll see him will be at the trial. Besides, I made a promise to Clay, and I fully intend on making good on it. We're going by the book on this one, right down to the bitter end if need be. Do you follow?"

Captain Meyers nodded indifferently, and looked at his watch. "When's the guy from Montgomery going to get here? I can't wait for him to get a load of this."

"He should be here within the hour." Butters stood and walked to the door. "If he's as good as everyone claims he is, we should be in good shape. You've heard the old saying 'too many cooks spoil the stew?' Well, that's not how it goes in detective work. You can never have too many good people breaking down stuff like this. Hopefully, he'll pick up on something that we've missed, or maybe he'll read something a little different. Never can tell."

Butters swirled his cup, watching the dregs rhythmically move with the coffee. "Oh and Jonas, just because we've asked a Bureau man down here to give us a second opinion don't give us a free ticket to take a nap. We aren't going to relax and let him have all the fun. Besides, you and I have cracked tough cases before, we might just get it all figured out before he does. That ought to make us look pretty good up in Montgomery, now wouldn't it?"

Both men smiled before the Sheriff issued the order. "Captain Meyers, take a few minutes to clear your head. Get a smoke, finish your coffee, call your wife and tell her you love her — do something else besides this case for a little while. When you've calmed down a bit, and feel good about it again, get back in there and keep that boy talking.

As long as he keeps talking, we are headed in the right direction."

***

Twenty minutes later, Captain Meyers walked back into the small room, placed a fresh cup of joe on the table, sat again in the uncomfortable chair, and opened the notebook to a page marked with a large paperclip. Nothing was said, and while he silently read, a column of smoke rose lazily from the cigarette hanging from his lip. He finished the first page, then the second, and shuffled through page after page, until skeptical eyes finally found the last thing he had written. It was chicken scratch, even for him, but he could still read it. He mouthed the words: "It's all a damn lie."

Meyers couldn't believe that it was real, but somehow it was all too real. John Bateman was just a kid, a seventeen-year-old kid who should be wondering who he was going to be taking to the prom in a few months, not sitting in a stuffy interrogation room, a couple of wrong answers away from being the prime suspect in a triple homicide. But that didn't change the fact that three men were dead — no they just weren't just dead, they had been brutally murdered, and as unlikely as it all seemed, every shred of evidence suggested this young man was most likely responsible.

For two and a half hours he'd listened to John tell the story. Yet, instead of getting closer to understanding what kind of depravity had actually occurred, he was both amused and shocked by what the kid's mind was able to produce . . . a bizarre, almost demonic tale, better suited for the plot of a horror film than a plausible explanation. The Captain shuttered in his chair thinking of what might lurk in the minds of today's youth, and what might have lurked, or was lurking still in the mind of this young man quietly sitting across the table from him. It was just reflex, but he brushed his hand across the place on his belt that usually held his holster. Butters had convinced him to leave the 9 millimeter on his desk, but now some small part of his psyche was wishing he had it back. Something strange had happened out there in the woods, Meyers was certain of that. He saw it in John's eyes the few times he had actually made eye contact during the questioning. Those eyes — there was something terrible hidden in those eyes.

Captain Meyers shifted uncomfortably in the chair, and was reaching for the notepad when the narrow door opened and a young deputy in corporal's stripes came across the room to the table, and whispered in Meyers' ear. While the deputy backed out of the room, the Captain crushed out his cigarette, and immediately reached into his shirt pocket and fished out a newly opened pack. Without looking, he pulled one, and tamped the filter three times on the table. He took a step back, produced a matchbook from his pants pocket, liberated one, and drug the tumescent end across the dark strip of rough paper along the bottom. The match crackled and flared, and he quickly waved it under the virgin end of the cigarette. Meyers watched John, expecting him to do something besides just sit there, but it seemed that staring at his lap was the only thing John Bateman was born to do. The Captain inhaled deeply and in the thick silence, the light hiss of burning tobacco joined the metallic movement of his ticking Timex.

A few minutes later, a knock on the door broke the silence. The deputy peeked in again. "Detective's ready for you, Captain." Meyers nodded and looked back at John and smiled. He knew this was going to be it. This was their chance to catch him in the lie. He had drug John Bateman through the whole story, not once, but twice, and the second time it had been nearly identical — almost verbatim. One of the first things they taught in Criminal Justice 101 was that nobody ever got the story right the second time, unless it had been rehearsed.

"Well, John. Looks like you'll have a chance to tell it one more time."

John looked up from his lap. His voice cracked, "Who are you going to get to listen to it this . . ." He stopped mid-sentence before continuing. "It really doesn't matter. You can get the mayor down here, the governor . . . hell, the president for that matter. I saw what I saw."

"Watch your mouth young man," Meyers said, "You are in enough trouble as it is, I don't want to have to call your father and tell him that on top of all this, you need your mouth washed out with soap too." Meyers stiffened in his seat, and the Sheriff's words came to him again, 'you need to tone it down just a little.' Meyers took a calming breath and casually flipped through the medical reports again. "We are bringing in a detective from the Bureau in Montgomery. His name is Jefferson Triplett."

John continued to look disinterested.

"You remember him don't you, John? He was all over the news maybe three years ago. He was the one who took down the Lieutenant Governor in that gambling ring. Remember when all that happened? If you like, you can tell him the same story you just told me, but I would strongly suggest telling the truth this time."

Meyers began to laugh, and John focused across the table on a man who was beginning to look more intimidating by the second. The end of the cigarette glowed red, as the Captain's barrel chest expanded. John swallowed hard and asked, "What are you laughing at now?"

"I'm laughing at you, John." Meyers stood and leaned forward, resting the palms of his hands in the middle of the table. The words rolled off his lips amid a shroud of light blue smoke, "Because I don't believe you can tell it the same way three times in a row."

Chapter 3

The interrogation room echoed nothingness. Alone, John sat quietly in that miserable wooden chair, dreading what was about to happen. They were going to make him wade through that horrible story again, and another dude with a badge was going to sit across the table from him and shake his head. Up until now he had controlled his emotions well, but that control seemed to be slowly eroding. One minute he felt calm and in complete control, believing there was no way they could make it his fault. The next, anxiety and fear of the unknown raged across his mind like a sweeping wildfire consuming an endless prairie. Negative thoughts came out of nowhere, one more negative than all the others put together: *What if they can find a way to make this my fault?*

Amid all the uncertainty, there was one thing he felt good about. No matter how scary or difficult the interviews were late yesterday or early this morning, no matter how difficult it was going to be in a few minutes with Detective Jefferson Triplett, at least for the moment he was safe. In the entire history of the Jessup County Sheriff's office, he might have been the only person who actually felt relieved to be inside that small uncomfortable room.

Despite what he felt and how well or poorly he was coping, one thing was slowly chipping away at his sanity. He had only been in the Sheriff's office since midday yesterday, fifteen hours at the most, and only four of those had been spent in questioning, but it all felt like eons to John. Between the gut spilling sessions, there was little to do except exercising his thumbs. Boredom slowly crept into his conscious from every direction, and the worried teen tried numerous things to pass the time. Singing, reciting poetry he had to memorize in school, he even went through the multiplication tables a few times. It quickly became a chore to think of anything but what had happened, and with it came those terrifying images he'd just as soon forget.

John's attention darted across the small room. He didn't know what he was looking for, but it just seemed to be the thing to do at the time. On his third sweep, he finally saw something besides the broken clock and the mirror screwed to the wall to his right. Coming through the ceiling tile, above the light fixture, he saw a bare copper wire. Too small to be coat hanger wire, he reasoned that it probably was used sometime in the past to anchor or power a recording device. It was exactly what he needed to see. With a new agenda, John started to examine the room for other covert paraphernalia he read about in the comic books and kid detective novels that wetted his appetite for reading when he was younger.

John scrutinized every nook and cranny. Up and down, back and forth along the walls, the trim, and the floor. He even slipped his hands under the table and ran sensitive fingers along the cracks and crevices searching for whatever they might have placed there to record the conversations. Nothing. Other than the relic hanging from the ceiling, the small room was clean and the very definition of boring.

Staring blankly ahead, he imagined what the observation room looked like behind the mirror. Two or three chairs, plain gray walls, possibly even a video camera capturing the interviews? What else could there be to it? He could not see them, but he could feel several sets of eyes staring at him through the glass. Dick Tracey, Sherlock Holmes, and Sigmund Freud were all there, making notes, and discussing how sick of a mind this kid must have. He wanted to make a face at the mirror, but decided not to. He didn't want to give Sigmund anything extra to analyze.

John noticed again the narrow door which brought uniforms and investigators into and out of his life without warning. That narrow door, for the moment, was closed, but John's flowing imagination soon had it opening up to the gleaming white light of the nut house Meyers mentioned earlier. But somewhere in the back of his mind, the worst case scenario blossomed. He was turning eighteen in a few months. If they didn't believe him and all this went to trial, the judge would surely decide to try him as an adult, and surely the jury would find him guilty of all the charges, all this insanity, and then surely that narrow door would open to the gleaming white light of a sparking electric chair.

The mental images of him convulsing while a lethal charge of electricity coursed through his body was a less than pleasant thought. He replaced the image of the electric chair, and the faint smell of burning hair that came with it, with a series of questions that needed answers.

Was the Captain right?
Have I completely lost it?

It doesn't seem possible, I don't think even rabies can make them go that crazy.

Am I the one going crazy, or am I already there?

The negative thoughts and questions came and went like summer thunderstorms, and he desperately tried to push them out of his mind. He wanted and needed to stay positive and in control. In a word, he needed to be . . . normal. He looked above the two-way mirror and saw the wall clock. When he was first introduced to the little room, John thought it was broken. With plenty of time to blow now, he studied it for a moment, and realized that the hands were running backwards! He watched, astounded, as the second hand ran smoothly backwards at what seemed to be a quicker than normal pace. He didn't know if it was his mind playing tricks on him, or if the Captain had set it up that way to shake up the interviewees. John watched for a few minutes, almost expecting the clock and possibly the whole wall to distort and melt like something out of a Dalí painting. Just when he thought he saw the hands of the clock starting to droop, the narrow door opened, and Meyers walked back in. Following him was a tall, slender fellow wearing a plain gray suit, presumably Detective Jefferson Triplett. Both men held items covered in clear plastic bags.

Meyers and the stranger sat the items on the table, and in the better light, John recognized his homemade primitive osage bow and his back quiver. Each was in separate bags marked 'evidence.' Before Triplett sat down, he laid two smaller bags on the table. In one was John's chamois camouflage shirt, and in the other, a single wooden arrow with dirty white fletching. It was his practice arrow — the one that he kept in his quiver to shoot at squirrels, leaves, and stumps while he was walking to and from his hunting spots.

Meyers lit another cigarette while Detective Triplett opened a small file folder and shuffled through some papers. The words: JESSUP COUNTY MURDERS, JANUARY 2, 1999 were written plainly on the tab. John watched Triplett's eyes moving back and forth over the papers before the man reached into his coat pocket, producing a moleskine notebook, and a custom-made pen. Triplett opened the notebook to the fabric book mark, scribbled a few lines of writing before clearing his throat.

"Good afternoon Mr. Bateman. My name is Jefferson Triplett. I am a detective with the Alabama Bureau of Investigation. ABI. Captain Meyers and I just spent a little time reviewing your file and your statement. He tells me you have seen some pretty remarkable things in the last few days. I believe that you are aware of what happened to the men in the pictures he showed you earlier. We are here to find out the truth about what happened. I think you can appreciate this — can't you Mr. Bateman?"

John nodded while Meyers made a poor attempt at a smoke ring.

"I understand you've told Captain Meyers what you saw at the hunting camp two times now, and he tells me that you remember what happened uncannily well."

"Detective Triplett —" John started to respond, but was interrupted.

"Please, call me Jeff."

The detective's informality caught John off guard. "Okay then, Mr. Triplett . . . uhm . . . I mean Jeff. When you've seen a wild animal do what I saw him do, a guy tends not to forget."

"Okay. Fair enough. If you don't mind Mr. Bateman—"

"Please Jeff, call me John."

Captain Meyers boiled out of his chair at what apparently sounded to him to be a smart-aleck remark, but before he could speak Detective Triplett coolly raised his hand signaling him to sit back down. Meyers silently complied, and huffed contemptuous and better built smoke rings into the air.

The presence of the new investigator made John nervous, not knowing exactly what he was in for, but after the loose introductions, he felt a little more at ease. At least this guy wasn't screaming at him.

"All right John," the detective said, "this is how I see us working through this. I'm going to ask you some questions about what happened this weekend. But don't worry, it's not going to be a long winded, sit down and tell it all again kind of session. I'm going to more or less guide you to and through the areas that I would like to know more about — sort of blocking it up into smaller important segments. Along the way, I may stop you and ask a few pertinent questions regarding what you recall. I'm going to try to keep that to a minimum, but just be ready for me to stop you with some questions along the way.

"When I ask a question, let's pretend to hit pause on your mind's playback, you answer the question and any follow-ups I or Captain Meyers may have for that particular response, then we can get back to wherever you were and continue with the statement . . . okay? All I ask of you is whatever part of the weekend we are in the process of dissecting, try to remember everything that happened. And I mean *everything*. It's imperative that we know what went on right down to the smallest detail. Also, please listen carefully to any questions I may ask, and really think about your answers before speaking. And remember, precision is a very good thing for us all right now. No one has ever gotten anywhere being vague, except maybe politicians, and as far as I know, nobody in this room is running for office. Are we good?"

John nodded.

"Very good. Now if you don't mind, let's take a stroll down memory lane together."

John shook his head. "I'm not sure it'll do any good. You aren't going to believe me. I hardly believe it myself." He paused, watching Triplett's facial expression for any signs of hope that he would be more open-minded than Meyers. Not seeing any, John said, "You know, I've been cooped up in either this metallic cracker box, or that stinking holding cell for almost an entire day now. I've told this story countless times unofficially, and two times to the Captain here on the record. There's just no other way to tell it. It's what I saw — it's what happened. Believe it or not."

***

Detective Triplett smiled. *This kid has a spine after all.*

He sat a little straighter in his chair, mentally adjusting what he wanted to say to match John's frame of mind. He had learned very early in his career that one of the quickest ways to earn a suspect's trust was to agree with him as much as possible. It also didn't hurt to make the conversation accommodating, instead of acidic and accusing. Unfortunately, that usually meant taking the long way around. Sometimes it worked, sometimes it didn't, but Triplett felt like it was worth the chance. He let the room fall silent for a moment before he glanced down at the table at the bagged evidence. A smile touched the corners of his mouth.

"Tell you what John, before we get into that, let's take care of something that's been bugging me since I first laid eyes on it. No. Wait a minute, bugging isn't the right word. Let's try fascinating. Why don't you tell me more about these things here on the table?"

Triplett glanced down at the bow and arrows between them. Although it wasn't strung, the smooth and elegant lines of the dark yellow osage wood were almost breathtaking. To stare at that wood bow was like staring directly into the past. "This is a genuine hand-made Indian-style bow, isn't it John? And the arrows — they look to be solid wood? I suppose these things are yours?"

John nodded and tried to smile.

Triplett's smile widened. "I don't think I've ever seen anyone hunting with stuff like this. Did you make them all yourself?"

John nodded again.

"Well, let's hear about it. Educate me about how one goes about carving a bow out of a piece of wood, and making genuine wood arrows."

Triplett cleverly offered the bait, and John bit down on it hard. For the first time since he walked through the doors of the Sheriff's Office, John opened up, free to talk about something that interested him. He quickly, yet intricately, started through the process of making a primitive bow and arrows, and how he hunted with them. Pleased that his plan worked, Detective Triplett opened the folder again. If there had been no mistakes when composing the report, this young man was no ordinary teenager — on paper, the kid was nothing less than a prodigy. He scanned through a few lines of information, and cast a skeptical eye across the table. Was everything he read about this young Mr. Bateman true? He was about to find out.

Chapter 4

From the file, Triplett saw that John Bateman was an honor student in high school who had taken several advanced courses, even a course in anatomy. Not many high school students could say that. He had been provisionally accepted to several headline universities. Alabama, Auburn, Ole Miss, and Florida State must have liked what they saw in this kid. But it was the last one on the list that impressed the detective the most. Vanderbilt! *Wow! They just don't let anyone go to school in Nashville.*

Each was promising some kind of scholarship, either in English or Journalism. John was young, but apparently, he exhibited a tremendous talent at the keyboard. By the time he was fifteen, he was editor of his school newspaper, and had sold a handful of freelance articles to *The Georgia Sportsman* and *Bowhunting Abroad*. It was clear to Detective Triplett that John was, indeed, an exceptional student, a gifted individual.

John's conversation was filling in the blanks where the file lacked. Detective Triplett suspected that John was active in the outdoors at an early age. The file did not mention that specifically, but John confirmed his suspicions during the first three minutes. Clayton Bateman, John's father, obviously was a huge influence during those early impressionable years. It was not uncommon for John to tag along with his father for walks in the woods, or to go hunting with him long before he was old enough to carry a weapon.

John was a model student and a natural in the woods. He quickly learned how being quiet and still meant everything, and the reward for his advanced abilities was quite a show in the wild. Deer, wild hogs, songbirds, hawks, rabbits, squirrels; in the woods, there were a lot of things a quiet boy could see. An interesting trait that Triplett picked up on right away was John's pure and sincere interests. The young man was the type that would revel over a Ruby-Throated Hummingbird sipping nectar from a blooming honeysuckle as much as he would a couple of impressive Whitetail bucks, battling for breeding rights. It didn't matter to him what they happened to stumble upon or what stumbled upon them in the woods, he was just happy to be there. Happy to be among wild things.

John elaborated on one hunt in particular that really sealed it for him. During the Thanksgiving holiday when he was seven, he and his father settled in a nice spot under a cedar tree on the downwind side of a food plot on their hunting club. The lessons of a hunter never seemed to end, and under that cedar, Clay told his eager young pupil that one of the most important things a hunter has in his bag of tricks are his two ears. Clay said, "There will be times, John, when your eyes will be useless. Something will be in the way, or it'll be too dark to see, or you will think you see something that isn't actually there. Those are the times when your ears will more than make up the difference. They will tell the story just as well, if not better than your eyes."

Clay had no sooner spoken those words, when footsteps sounded in the dry leaves in the woods on the other side of the field. The footsteps advanced, but there was something else. It was a slight ticking sound, faint but audible, barely heard over the crunching dry leaves. Smiling, Clay asked John if he heard it, but the excited adolescent could only hear the louder and more pronounced footsteps. Clay told him to listen closely, and to try to remove what he already heard, focusing on the sounds that might be there if the crunching dry leaves were silent. It took a few minutes, but compartmentalizing the footfalls helped as the light ticking sound became the only thing John could hear.

The young hunter, not knowing what that meant, watched his father carefully working the action on the Winchester. The footsteps continued, and seemed to be right in their laps when a large buck stepped from the brush into the field. "It was his antlers," his father whispered to him out of the corner of his mouth. "His antlers were bumping and popping the limbs in the brush." Clay Bateman realized it was a buck long before he ever laid eyes on it.

The listening lesson could not have come at a better time, and both father and son were thrilled at the sight of the large buck nibbling on the lush rye grass. It was getting late, and the evening's light was starting to fade, but they both could still easily see the creamy white antlers high above the buck's dark gray head. He didn't flinch when the rifle split the still evening air, and when the blur from the explosion settled, the largest buck John had ever seen lay in the edge of the field some eighty yards away. From that moment, God could have written the eleventh commandment: *John Bateman will be a hunter.*

John's development with weapons was equally predictable. A twenty-gauge shotgun at ten, 30-30 rifle when he was twelve, compound bow when he was thirteen.

Right away, John showed a natural, almost uncanny ability with the bow. During his first bowhunting season, he became the proud owner of the Alabama state youth record for whitetail deer, arrowing a fine 128 3/8^{ths} inch typical nine pointer during the Christmas holidays.

Another fruitful year went by before John's choice in weaponry would ironically regress. He and Clay were at the big deer exposition show in Birmingham when he first saw it. An older man standing in line to shoot the archery targets was cradling something that John had only seen in old magazines, and on a wall display at a sporting goods store in Mobile. For the first time, he came face to face with a working recurve bow.

John sat and watched, mesmerized as the gentleman fluidly drew and shot it twenty five times at the standard circular targets downrange. He was immediately drawn to the weapon, and admired how quiet and how powerful it seemed. How could anyone shoot a bow instinctively without sights? The fellow spent a few minutes with him and explained that it was much like throwing a baseball or shooting a basketball. It took practice, practice, and more practice, but eventually the shots would just come. The archer would subconsciously know where to hold the bow in order to make shots at most any distance, even at moving targets. His new friend went back through the targets a second time, and John was totally enamored. The entire process seemed effortless, and the challenge of becoming proficient with a more primitive hunting weapon naturally appealed to him.

The next spring, using money he made from mowing lawns, John bought an old Bear Kodiak recurve. It was a lightweight bow, only registering thirty-eight pounds at his shorter draw length, and after some ribbing from the peanut gallery about shooting what they called a child's toy, he matched it perfectly with a set of forgotten aluminum arrows he found in the backroom of the local bow shop. The arrows flew straight and true, and for John, it was love at first shot.

The following fall, he hunted the entire bow season with that lightweight recurve. He had a couple of discouraging misses early on, but finally he managed to hold his nerves together long enough to arrow a fat doe. It was a close shot, less than ten yards, and the perfectly placed arrow punctured both lungs and sliced open the animal's aorta. She was dead before she took the first bound. The kill sent a surge of adrenaline though his system, feeding the need and desire to hunt with the more primitive version of his compound bow.

That Christmas, one of John's stocking stuffers was a book about the hunting habits of Native Americans. The pages spoke to him, and immediately he started thinking of how hunting used to be during those times. Not necessarily the methods they used, such as herding animals off cliffs. That kind of primitive hunting seemed a bit too brutal, but more so the nature of the primitive weapons, specifically bows, they used.

The book was a wealth of information, and showcased the entire process, literally going from limbs or logs of trees all the way to the finished product. John was fascinated with the pictures of bows in different stages of production. Freshly split logs turned into blocky staves, and those staves, after some care and attention from draw knives and rasps, slowly turned into long slender pieces of refined wood. The process continued, steadily carving and scraping the limbs, getting them to bend evenly when drawn. The entire process seemed mystical, and John was once again in love.

When he read the last word on the last page of that book, he knew that his next challenge would be making and hunting with his own primitive archery tackle. To John, it was the hopelessly irresistible call of the Sirens, and there on the table between him and Detective Triplett was his best bow yet. It was a straight and clean piece of osage without a knot, blemish, or erroneous swirl of grain on it anywhere from tip to tip. Neither investigator could appreciate exactly how remarkable that bow was. There literally wasn't another one like it in the world. John smiled as he talked about whittling it down to size, and getting those long limbs to bend just right. It had been a daunting task, but the final result was a stunning masterpiece of functional art, a formidable weapon worthy of the deed for which it was designed.

Killing.

Chapter 5

Detective Triplett listened to the teenager's story. Just as he planned, John was revealing volumes about himself and his personality, but he had not bargained on the impromptu education he was receiving on the nuances of primitive bowhunting. The detective was fascinated at John's explanation, but trying to take it all in and somehow link it to the murders wasn't connecting. It was an interesting concept, and the detective could appreciate the challenge involved, but there was something about the process that didn't seem logical or desirable. Maybe there was something embedded in the whole primitive state of hunting that might nudge a kid into some evil game of bloodlust?

"John, I'm not sure I follow you here. I mean, I think I get why you like hunting with bows. I see that it's a heckuva challenge compared to rifles and such, and it gives you something new and fresh to write about, but why go so far as to hunt with recurves and even these primitive bows? Don't you think you are limiting yourself too much? The whole point of hunting is to kill something, right?"

"That's just it, detective." John smiled. "I like the limitations — the challenge. I like the idea of getting close enough to see them blink, and they not know I'm there. You know for bowhunters, the closer you get to em' the more exciting it is."

Triplett, trying to maintain a neutral facial expression, was screaming on the inside. He was sure that John had just stumbled, and that small, harmless, almost nondescript sentence was something important that no one else had heard him say.

'The closer you get to em' the more exciting it is.'

There was no way of knowing for sure, but this was the first thing that John had said that could even remotely be used to start to explain what happened. Those three guys were friends of his, and by very definition, he had to be close to them. He knew it was too simple, but it was a start.

Triplett tried to play it cool, and tapped his finger on the desk — thinking. "I see. But don't you miss chances when you limit yourself to shots so close?"

"Sure. The odds are absolutely in the game's favor. Comparatively speaking, the chances of getting a shot are very low for me, but it's what I do with the chances I do get that count the most. For the most part, almost everyone that ventures into the woods these days is only looking for big antlers. So they maximize their weapons, and then minimize their opportunity, because those kind of bucks aren't hiding behind every tree in the woods. These folks might see only one deer a season that they think is worth killing. I'm the opposite. I minimize what I hunt with, and then maximize the opportunity."

Triplett could still hear the chilling statement. *'The closer you get to em' the more exciting it is.'* He was trying hard to connect more dots from the conversation, but it seemed that one high note had dissipated into the flat hum of what he considered to be a dissertation on hunting methods.

John continued. "These folks just want to kill the biggest buck out there and scoff at the rest of them, good opportunities or not. Hunting deer and not shooting . . .

that's limiting the opportunity." John pointed at his bow on the table. "Hunting with a bow like this, I have to be better than the best hunter out there. I work hard to position myself perfectly along a trail, at a food source, or in a pinch point to get a good shot at the ranges I'm comfortable with. With this bow, it's about twenty yards, maybe a little further, so I feel pretty good shooting does and smaller bucks that I can get close enough to and make a good shot on."

John shrugged his shoulders, "Sure, I might let a few small ones walk if I've already downed a decent buck, but if the conditions are right, and if a chance to kill happens —"

Detective Triplett finished his sentence. "You maximize the opportunity."

John smiled again. "Exactly."

The detective sat back in his chair and continued to listen. The file had told him a lot about this kid, but the conversation, straight from John's own mouth, was accounting for things the paperwork could not easily provide, specifically his own psychological state, personal drive, and ego.

To untrained ears, John's oratory might seem unimportant. But in reality, all investigations started out this way. Triplett considered himself a good detective, and all good detectives know that all good investigations started out with a blank canvas, a few brushes, and just a handful of paint. In the beginning there are few brush strokes, and few colors, but over time paint is mixed, and more and more stokes are made. As the process continues, those few brushes lay hundreds, sometimes thousands of strokes using dozens of colors made from just a few given at the beginning. And in the end, the painting is there to admire — sometimes a masterpiece, sometimes not. What Detective Triplett was doing now was applying the very important first strokes; laying a foundation for the image that would soon find its way onto the canvas.

Triplett also was a big advocate of the axiom that most of the time, the simplest explanation is usually right. Even though John was an extraordinary kid, he was still a kid. The detective had already considered that all this would somehow stem from something that plagued every teenager. Stress at school, peer pressure, girls, drugs, or possibly something unique to John — deadline pressures. Deadlines at school were one thing, but professional deadlines in the literary world were something entirely different. John would be subject to both, and that in itself might have caused him to abandon reality.

Detective Triplett didn't know exactly what he was looking for to help him paint the picture, but he realized that whatever it was would probably come in small pieces. The statement: *'The closer you get to em' the more exciting it is'* was a good start.

The detective carefully digested John's words, all the while making light strokes on the canvas with his paints and brushes. He was trying to form a profile that could be classified by either law enforcement, or psychiatric professionals. It wasn't easy. Other than the primitive hunting fetish, and his uncanny writing abilities, John seemed about as normal as they come. It was also obvious to Triplett that John was a guy that relished a challenge. Scholarly, and semi-professionally, John was at the top of his class, and had enjoyed success competing against the best outdoor writers in the region, and in some cases the country. John's list of publications was growing, and so was his passion for the art of composition. Detective Triplett could easily see and hear it in John's face and voice. And when he wasn't busy with school or writing, his hobbies reflected the same fervor. Yet the challenge did not seem to come from other sportsmen trying to top his records. What drove him was the challenge to hunt as effectively and as efficiently as possible — man against nature. The desire to accomplish what others have not or could not seemed to be what he liked. He transferred this to his extracurricular and outdoor pursuits, eventually gravitating to hunting with primitive weapons in a world that catered towards a modern flair.

Detective Triplett creased down a fresh page in his notebook and wrote:

JB is an overachiever — his favorite pastime has become boring. So much so that he's switched from modern weaponry to primitive means. He brings himself down to the most primitive level imaginable, and still is able to kill his quarry, on the quarry's terms, not his. The closer you get to em' the more exciting it is! John Bateman is a killer . . . Murderer . . . Maybe?!?

That last line was suspect. Despite what he heard and wrote, Triplett knew that none of it made John a murderer. A ramped-up eccentric teenager consumed with the hunt, and writing about it — maybe — but not a murderer. Nothing from his past suggested a psyche-changing occurrence, mental instability, or anything that might otherwise tip-off anger or violence towards his father's friends. If anything, John seemed to be living out every young man's dream. He came from a good family, was probably going to get most if not all of his college education paid for, and have a nice job waiting on him right out of school at a career-building newspaper, or outdoor magazine. Triplett actually started to feel envious. It was strange to admit, but that something John Bateman so easily possessed at a very early age eluded all but very few adults, a complete and encompassing drive to excel.

Triplett continued writing.

Why would JB want to kill these men . . . Motive? Three friends on a regular hunting trip? Maybe deer just didn't do it for him anymore . . . Bored??? Maybe he needed to hunt something other than wildlife? Something smarter than deer. Something that would hunt him back? The closer you get to em' the more exciting it is!

Questions were starting to fill pages in his notebook. Questions that did not have answers.

Chapter 6

Forty-five minutes into the interview Triplett found himself face to face with another reality. It was hard not to *like* John. The detective had not ascended to the top of his profession without the ability to judge people, more or less, from conversation and body language. He took pride in it, and most would say he was good at it, although some of his colleagues considered that type of 'gut feeling' pure hokum. Triplett knew the young man sitting across from him was intelligent, well spoken, and generally friendly, but then again, so were Bundy and Dahmer.

Despite the appeal, he couldn't ignore that all the information collected by the Sheriff's Department was damning. Every bit of evidence pointed towards what happened in the back woods of southern Jessup County was something resembling a chapter out of *The Most Dangerous Game*. Three men were dead, all killed at the hunting camp from apparent arrow wounds, and there was John Bateman, the only bowhunter in camp, walking away from it all with just a few scratches, spouting an unbelievable story, and shamelessly harboring a bloody shirt-tail along with a bloody arrow in his quiver. No matter how likeable John was, the blood could not be ignored.

John finished talking, and Detective Triplett saw the teen staring at his bow like an old friend. He took another chance. "Hey John, would you care if I tried to draw your bow? How do you go about stringing it?" He motioned approvingly at the bow, and John at once had it free of its plastic prison, running his hands down the limbs checking for any mistreatment. There was none, and John grasped the bow by the handle with his right hand, and with the other, he secured the string loop on the grooves at the lower limb tip. He twisted the bow in his hands so that the target side was facing him, and wedged the bottom limb tip against the arch of his right foot. John's left hand caught the top string loop, and ran it up the limb as far as it would go. Then pulling the handle with his right hand, while pushing the top limb with his left, the limbs gently arced, allowing him to slide the top loop into place on the upper limb tip's string groove. In a whisper the bow was strung. Both investigators' eyes widened at the ease at which the teen had made the bow ready to fire.

John handed the bow to Triplett. "Here ya go detective. She's not that rank — came out to fifty-eight pounds at my draw. You need to be careful though. Not supposed to draw them back further than they are used to. It's a sure way to blow one apart." John considered the detective's height, arm length, and build. "Looks like your frame is a touch bigger than mine. If you don't mind, just to be safe, don't draw it back much past your mouth and it'll be okay. Oh, and be sure not to let it go without an arrow in her. I'd rather you run over it with your squad car than to dry-fire her."

Triplett held the handle in his left hand, and after a couple of short warm up draws, feeling where the resistance began, he slowly started pulling. He almost made it to his mouth when the string stopped. His left arm quivered for a moment, fighting the resistance, and then he slowly let it back down. The detective was amazed at how strong the simple wood bow was, and getting a better grip, he tried to draw it again. The string stopped quicker the second time. Flummoxed, Triplett eased the string down, and tried to hand the bow to Meyers. The Captain, who looked as if he was expecting ether the bow or the man drawing it to break, shook his head. "I haven't drawn a bow since I was a kid, back when I had one of those little green fiberglass jobs you could get at the dime store. Besides, I hurt my shoulder back in the academy trying to run down an overzealous major pretending to be a suspect fleeing on foot. I don't think I need to risk re-injuring it pulling back a silly bow."

***

After the show and tell session was over, both Triplett and Meyers suggested a small break. Another deputy escorted John to the bathroom down the hall, and both investigators walked back to Meyers' office. They barely made it through the door when Sheriff Butters stuck his head inside. Smiling, he said, "Y'all through rattling his cage already?"

Captain Meyers said, "Detective Jefferson Triplett, this is my boss, Sheriff David Butters."

Triplett extended his hand, "Pleased to meet you, Sheriff."

"Yeah, yeah, yeah," Butters said dryly. "Let's forget the proprieties for now, and get right to it." He hooked a thumb over his shoulder towards the restrooms where the person of interest was presumably emptying his bladder. "So what do you think of our young hunter so far?"

"Well, there's not too much to say at the moment. I wanted to try and make him comfortable and just get him going, so I got him to tell me a little about himself, his background, et cetera. I was hoping that he'd give me something — the beginnings of a profile, perhaps. I can certainty tell you one thing though. This young man seems to be quite an exceptional fellow. I don't think I've ever met a teenager that is as well-spoken as he is."

The Sheriff leaned on the edge of Meyers' desk, and twisted his mustache. "He's sharp. There's no denying that. Sometimes those are the kind that will fool you the most. That's the reason you're here — you're supposed to be one of the best in Montgomery. When I made the call, everyone there told me you were the man for the job." Butters paused and looked over the Captain's messy desk. He appeared to suppress the desire to say something about it, opting to stay on track with the conversation. "You know, he seems to be everything you'd want to see in a kid. I'm not sure how to put it without sounding judgmental, but most of them these days are either on something, or just plain weird. We've seen it down here, so I know you've seen it in Montgomery. They sure do mess up big time when they start rolling those left handed cigarettes, and sniffing the white powder. I'm not sure if that's what going on here or not. Heck, he might just be off his rocker. There could very well be some demons running around inside that boy's head, slowly breaking him. We've seen that before too." He looked again at Detective Triplett, "You're supposed to help us figure out which one it is."

The detective nodded. "I think I'll be able to help, as long as we can keep him talking. If he's talking, he'll eventually slip up and tell us something that he shouldn't, or tell us something inconsistent with the earlier statements Captain Meyers recorded. If he's hiding something, or an addict, or maybe even mentally ill, in time it always comes out. He's told us quite a bit about himself already, so when we get back into what happened down there in the woods, it'll be easier to catch things that seem counter to his personality. And if he's bipolar, we'll just have to wait until the other kid inside him gets bored with all the monotonous repetition, and decides to join in the fun."

"Well, you two know what to do, so get in there and do it. Let's see what he says this time." The Sheriff scratched his cheek. "I've been watching some from behind the mirror. There were a few times he looked a little rattled, but for the most part, he seems to be in control. And I'm really surprised that he's as steady as he is. Most kids I know his age would have folded in ten minutes especially with Jonas's foot on the gas pedal. You might know something about interrogation procedures we don't, but if you ask me, I think we need to keep it simple. Simple and calm. Especially since this kid is no ordinary kid."

Detective Triplett nodded. "That's exactly what I had in mind."

Butters motioned to his second in command, and Meyers quickly stepped to the door and hollered down the hall to the deputy who was stationed outside of the men's room. "Time's up. Let's get him back in there."

Part II

Chapter 1

"John Bateman," I said to the small mirror in the men's room, "you're in big trouble." The ragged guy looking back at me in that borrowed, bright orange county jail jumpsuit just sat there staring. If reflections could speak, I am sure he would say, "You're absolutely right, Johnny boy!"

I double cupped hands under the spigot, splashed cold water on my face and looked again, but the guy in the mirror still wasn't talking. Toweling the water away, I wondered about this new man named Jefferson Triplett. He wasn't like the Captain. A little kinder, a little gentler, maybe, but there still was an aura about him that I didn't like. He hadn't asked me to dive right into what happened at camp — no, the detective first wanted to know more about me. How I grew up, my schooling and hobbies, what made me tick, and the only reason he would be interested in all that is because he was trying to label me. He wanted to put me in a neat little box with 'psycho,' or 'bipolar,' or maybe simply 'damaged' stamped on the top, tie a bow on it, and present it to the Judge. I hadn't given him what he wanted though, and for the first time in my life, someone being disappointed in me was a good thing.

The door opened and the deputy told me to hurry up, they were ready to go again, and on the short walk down the hallway, I tried to see the bright side. Despite all the negative connotations he probably sensed from Meyers, our little chat so far had gone well. At times, it felt like the detective was actually pulling for me. I could tell he liked my selfbow and was impressed with my writing abilities, but with the preliminaries over, there was nothing left to do but sing the rest of the song. God only knows what he'd think of me then.

I sat back down at the table and took a deep breath. The bathroom break actually helped. My bladder was back to its normal size, and even though the air down the hallway was still stale and smelled of burnt coffee, it was far better than the acrid clouds leaking from those stinking cigarettes. The clean air was cool and crisp in my lungs, but that and the brief change of scenery hadn't helped me answer a very important question floating around inside my head. How was I going to get him to believe me? While I waited and wondered, I noticed that little room began to feel a little better, bigger perhaps, but all that changed when Meyers led Triplett back through that narrow door.

"Okay, John," Detective Triplett said, smiling. "So far we are doing very well. We've covered some of what I wanted to talk about, and I've got a good handle on who you are. Now it's time for you to buckle down and walk me through what happened down there. Don't worry about getting in a hurry; let's just take this one step at a time. I just borrowed a fresh pen from Captain Meyers, I've turned to a fresh page in my notebook, and my fingers are all limbered up. Whenever you are ready."

The smile looked fake and I caught a hint of glum in his voice, but he was right. There was no need to keep them or me waiting, it was time to get it over with — the quicker the better. After a good long deep breath, I asked, "Where would you like me to start?"

Triplett said, "I've been thinking about that. An hour ago I would have said let's start at the beginning, but I don't think that will be necessary." He flipped back a couple of pages in Meyers' notebook, and ran a finger across a page. "How about a little about the hunting club to start. That, and why your father didn't go hunting with you."

So I nodded and started the story again.

"Dad and I hunt with a few other guys he grew up with down in the southern part of the county. Dad, me, Al, Renn, and Kirby — we call it the Indian Mound Creek Hunting Club. It's just a small club, nothing fancy, and we hunt on Al Rutledge's family land. We've been doing this New Year's deer hunt for as long as I remember. The rut usually is just starting in early January, and being in the woods with doe-crazy bucks usually makes for good hunting.

"We were up early New Year's Day. Mom was starting the black-eyed peas for lunch and dad and I were prepping and gathering gear for the week when the phone rang. It was Jim Elliott, Dad's boss. Dad's a regional manager for Gulf Pharmaceuticals, and it didn't take me long to realize that he wasn't going hunting. There was a mix-up at the St. Louis warehouse — a botched drug shipment or something, and the way Mr. Elliott was screaming on the other end of the line, it had to be a big one.

"Mom always wanted to see the arch, so around 10:00, they pulled out of the driveway with a 737 waiting for them in Birmingham . . . next stop St. Louis. Before they left, I tried to get him to shuffle the work to someone else. He wasn't the only one who worked for them. I even tried to throw Kirby under the bus. But dad wouldn't have it. He said that Kirby had handled some problems in the Mobile and Pensacola offices the last quarter, and that the big bosses in Memphis wanted this particularly sensitive matter handled quickly, and they wanted the regional manager on it ASAP.

"About an hour after they left, it was Kirby instead of Al who pulled in the driveway. Al was helping Renn with some last minute preparations, and it was just easier for Kirby to swing by. I managed to pack all my stuff in the back of his already over-loaded Suburban, and we met Al and Renn in Montgomery for lunch before caravanning south. It would have been better with Al. Kirby wasn't my favorite person, a little too interested in himself at times, but it wasn't a terrible ride down. He bought a few of those new motion activated game cameras sometime back in the fall, and I had a blast looking at all the pictures. He told me he had one of a buck that was sure to break the Alabama record, and might give the world record a run for its money. I thought he was full of it until he handed me another stack of pictures."

Detective Triplett said, "That's when you first saw the picture of the big twelve pointer with the drop tine?"

"Exactly. He had been framed by one of the cameras twice in the same night. A freaking monster! I figured that nobody would ever see him again. Dad and Al used to joke that really big deer didn't get big being stupid, but the rut has a way of evening things up a little. If we were ever going to see him, it would be during the rut. I think I stared at that picture the rest of the way down, I don't even remember going through Halifax. But when we pulled in the driveway, I heard Kirby gasp, and right away we could tell that something was wrong."

Triplett looked up from his notebook. "How so?"

"We have a neat set up down there. Several years ago dad and the guys decided to pool their resources, and they built a small camp house. Two bedrooms, living room, bathroom, a small kitchen, and all the stuff that goes along with it. It wasn't camping to me, but the codgers seemed to like it okay. The last thing they added to it was a nice covered front porch. When we pulled into the drive, everything we kept on it was torn and scattered. The big aerial photo map of the place we had under Plexiglas was broken off and tossed, the bragging board was busted and the pictures scattered all over the porch. The Webber grill was in the yard with several big dents and cracks in it. The wooden frames that held the map and the bragging board were splintered."

"And you thought the neighboring hunting club was responsible? A prank of sorts?"

"The guys didn't at first. My girlfriend, Marissa, and I came down in mid-December, right after school got out. I had just finished my osage bow, and wanted to hunt a morning with it, but we ended up mostly scouting out new hunting areas, trying to find a couple of places I could hunt with it. I promised a story about my first selfbow kill to the editor at Traditional Bowhunter Magazine, and I didn't really have a go-to hunting spot suited for a short range bow. But the guys just thought that she and I had a real interesting half a day to ourselves down here." I smiled and could feel a warmth come to my cheeks. "If you get my drift."

"Yeah, I get your drift." Triplett pointed at a place in the notebook. "I see a direct quote from Captain Meyers that in your prior statement, Renn said, 'Damn Johnny-boy, that wildcat you're dating must like it rough.'"

I could feel my face getting warmer. "That's what he said, but it isn't like that. She and I haven't been dating long, and she can nearly out-walk me in the woods. I think she likes hunting more than I do. It took a little bit of convincing, but I finally got them to quit ribbing me about it. So we were all standing around scratching our heads, and then Al saw the dents on the door."

"The camp house door?"

I nodded. "The camp house wasn't broken into, but somebody had worked the door over pretty good. In the center of each dent was smeared mud print that was shaped like a deer hoof. We all laughed at the first thing that came to our minds, so the next best explanation was that it must have been guys from the other club."

"Yeah." Detective Triplett glanced at Meyers. "I hear there's a history between you and the — what is it called? The Big Oak Hunting Club. You all do seem to have an interesting rapport with them. Captain Meyers told me about one of the more colorful exchanges a few years ago. I believe they started it with the coon dog dung in the coveralls prank, and you all retaliated with roadkill stew under their camp trailer."

I actually started laughing thinking about it. "Yeah, we spent two days picking up half rotten coons, coyotes, and possums off the road, and then, I think it was a Wednesday night, we snuck into their camp, loosened the trailer skirts, and scattered about seventy-five pounds of mangled rotting critters under it. It had two whole days to cook under there, and I heard that when Donnie and the boys showed up Friday afternoon they all puked. We laughed about it until we cried. They must have thought a whole family of raccoons, in-laws included, must have decided that life wasn't worth living anymore, and dug under the trailer and committed some kind of mass suicide."

Triplett shook his head, almost laughing. "And this Donnie was Donnie Abernathy, right? The president of the neighboring hunt club?" Triplett glanced again at the paper. "The Big Oak Hunt Club?"

"Yes, yes, and yes. Their club land touches the Rutledge property on the east side — their camp is a mile and a half, maybe two from ours as the crow flies. Most of the guys that hunt over there grew up with Al, Renn, and dad here in Jessup County."

"What about Kirby McNeil? You didn't mention him."

"Dad invited Kirby to start hunting with us after he began work with dad's company. He grew up down close to the beach. Foley, I believe."

Detective Triplett continued to make notes, then looked at John and said, "If most all of them knew one another, I assume you were well received? What I mean, John, is that you are an entire generation younger than the rest of the members. How well did you know and get along with the others?"

"They were mainly dad's friends, and because they were his friends, they were my friends. Some were closer than others, but down in this neck of the woods, it's hard not to be friendly with nearly everyone. Folks that live twenty miles apart call each other neighbors at the grocery store."

Triplett pointed to the notebook, "It says here you dated somebody that was related to Donnie Abernathy for a while."

"I did. Last year, for a little bit. Her name was Josey Abernathy. Donnie's niece. She was nice enough, but way too much drama. It didn't last long, and right after we broke up she threatened to ruin my life. I told her I didn't care, and the next day she practically announced to the whole school that I had knocked her up. Well, a day or two later Donnie caught up with me in town and suggested that I watch my back by giving me a two fingered pistol salute. Then two weeks later, she wound up in a bad car wreck coming home from a slumber party of sorts that one of her friends had down in Mobile — the kind of slumber party that funnels beers instead of having pillow fights. She ended up wrapping her Camaro around the largest utility pole on I-65 just a few miles south of Montgomery. The medical examiner confirmed that she was lying about being pregnant, but Donnie just never let it go and always blamed me. Said I drove her to it."

Triplett's face suddenly changed. He glanced at Meyers, then back to me and said, "Were the guys from the Big Oak hunting this weekend too?"

I said, "I dunno. We thought they pulled another gag on us Saturday at lunch with a doe I got that morning, but they didn't claim responsibility. If they were hunting, we didn't hear anything out of them."

Detective Triplett turned back to Meyers. "Has anyone checked on this? Seems like a long shot, but if Donnie never got over losing his niece, he might have done something. I've seen people killed over less."

For the first time that day, Captain Jonas Meyers didn't have an answer. He looked like he'd been strapped to a chair and forced to watch someone kick his dog. He blinked several times before standing and walking to the narrow door. "We sure haven't, detective, but I promise you we'll know within the hour."

Chapter 2

When Captain Meyers returned, he was holding three Cokes. He sat one in front of Triplett, then sat one on the table in front of me. I opened mine, and took a sip and made a face. Hot. Triplett grabbed his and started to open it, but didn't. I guess he didn't like them hot either.

The detective folded his hands together on the table and said, "So John, the camp is busted up some and there are fake deer tracks in the dents on the door. Let's move on from there. Tell me about when you saw the big buck."

I nodded. "Well, we spent a few minutes cleaning up some, trying to hurry up so we could salvage a late evening hunt. It took longer than we thought, but late or not, Al, Renn, and I decided to hit the woods. The wind was wrong for the two stands I really wanted to hunt, the ones that Marissa and I set, so Al invited me to sit in one of his. We loaded our stuff and —"

"Wait a second John," Triplett said. "You didn't mention Kirby?"

"He said the wind was wrong for his stands too. Before we left for the woods, he mentioned something about delivering a late Christmas present to an Aunt of his down in Pike County . . . said he was going to do that, and would be back in time to help us drag anything out of the woods if we were lucky enough to kill something."

Triplett wrote again in his notebook and said, "Strange that he was excited about having a potential record setting buck in the pictures, yet opted to not hunt."

Captain Meyers cleared his throat and said, "I thought the same thing too, but I've ruined good hunting spots before by being too hasty. Let a buck catch your sent on the wrong wind, or see you walking to your spot and that's it . . . no more buck."

I agreed, "Me too. I figured he was just trying to play it safe. I guess we didn't care about the risk, and just went hunting. We didn't kill anything, but it was a very interesting evening. When it was dark, we met back at the truck. Each of us had seen a huge buck, and after we told the stories, we couldn't believe it. The consensus was that we all saw the massive twelve pointer from Kirby's game camera pictures.

"Renn hunted the most remote stand and saw him first at 5:40. He said the deer was partly hidden in a tangle of vines, and somehow spotted him in the stand. The deer watched him for a minute or two then bounded away down the creek. I saw him next, six minutes later. I caught movement, and glimpsed him slipping down the creek. I could have killed him with a rifle easy, but I only had my bow. He stopped and looked straight at me, then quickly moved on. Then Al saw him five minutes later at 5:51. Al said he trotted by the food plot, and stopped and looked at him too. He said he was just fifty yards away, but was still elusive enough to keep trees and limbs between them, not giving him a clear lane to shoot through. Al laughed and said that even if there had been an opening, it was doubtful that he could have managed a shot — terminal case of buck fever. It was hard to believe that the same deer would visit each of us across that distance . . . almost a mile and a half."

I stopped for a moment, waiting to see if any of this had raised a red flag with the detective. Apparently it hadn't. He glanced back and forth between me and his notebook a few times while he finished with whatever notes he was writing. When he realized I was just staring at him, he straightened in his chair, and tapped the pen on his lower lip a few times. He might not have completely caught it, but something was bugging him.

He finally said, "You're stressing this so you must think it's really important, but I don't get it. You really think it was just one deer? You said there were a bunch of big deer on those trail camera pictures. Maybe it could have been three separate deer that just looked alike? And another thing, how was the timeline established? How do you know you saw him exactly at those times?"

I knew then that Triplett wasn't a hunter. I glanced at Captain Meyers and he was shaking his head. I didn't know if he was reacting that way because he didn't believe me, or at Triplett for not understanding.

Before I could answer Meyers scratched his forehead and said, "I can answer the timeline question, detective. Indian Mound Hunt Club usually keeps a pretty tight ship at deer camp. As weird as it sounds, they actually do synchronize watches when they're down there. Clay Bateman was in the Army — Rangers I believe, and he always superimposed some of the things he learned at Fort Benning on the guys when they were down there hunting. I've hunted with Clay before, and at times, it was like being in basic training.

"Now, as far as the deer goes, even a fawn can make a mile and a half in eleven minutes. Could probably do it with a hoof tied behind its back. But big or small, young or old, none are going to do it without one heckuva good reason."

The detective shrugged his shoulders. "What kind of reason would he have?"

"A deer that's being pushed by dogs or coyotes could easily do such a thing, but one that is just out for a leisurely stroll won't. They also run pretty hard during the rut chasing she-deer, but in all the years I've seen this happen, I've never seen them run in a straight line. Oh, I imagine a horny buck hoping to get his pecker wet probably wouldn't mind running hard for ten miles in a straight line, but the only way he'd do it is if that hot little hussy in front of him does it first. I'll nearly bet the farm that a doe in estrous, being chased by a rutting buck has *never* covered any amount of ground in a straight line. And according to John here, no one saw a doe anywhere near the buck anyways . . . nor dogs, nor coyotes."

Meyers took a moment to light another Marlboro before continuing, "John here thinks it was the same deer, since it was supposedly wearing the same set of antlers. He also thinks that Mr. Twelve-pointer had a good reason for covering that kind of ground." Meyers pointed a big accusing finger at me, "Go ahead John, tell the detective what you think he was doing."

I stared at Triplett, silently praying. Everything up till now had been reasonable, and more importantly, explainable. But what I was about to say was going to do it. It was going to splatter the last remaining shreds of my credibility all over the floor like an over-ripe watermelon falling off a truck. I looked at my lap and sighed and thought about how I could say it and not sound like an escapee from a mental hospital. Nothing came to me, so I just closed my eyes and said it.

"Well, it didn't make any sense at the time, but after seeing it all unfold, especially after what happened Saturday evening, I think there was a good reason for the way that buck walked. He wasn't just taking a stroll or chasing females. He was scouting. Scouting *us!*"

Detective Triplett's jaw dropped. He looked at me for a moment before deliberately blinking a few times. Almost laughing, he said, "Did I just hear you right? You think that this deer was — somehow — looking for you?"

"Not just me. He was scouting the others too, all of us." I moved my finger back and forth between them a few times. "What you two are missing here is this buck wasn't acting right; he didn't look normal at all. It's like he had it all planned. Like he knew we were going to be there."

Triplett still looked shocked. "Come on, John. It's true that I'm not much of an outdoorsman, but I've seen enough National Geographic specials to know that very few things in North America pose much of a threat to us. A grumpy grizzly, maybe a mama black bear if you screw with her cubs, I've heard of a few moose stomping hunters that have gotten too close, and maybe a mountain lion scratching up a few folks here and there . . . but a Whitetail deer?" Triplett's eyes rolled towards the ceiling, a look of sheer disgust. The Captain watched him, smiling, and then made the end of his Marlboro glow red.

There was nothing I could do. I couldn't save it. Triplett had just probably written me off, and with Meyers in his hip pocket, this whole thing seemed to be circling the drain. I almost panicked, but after a few deep breaths, I thought of something to say. It wasn't going to be what they wanted to hear, but I sure needed it.

I stood and stared right into the detective's twinkling blue eyes and said, "It didn't seem like he was watching us at first, it just seemed, well, a little weird. But after what happened Saturday, I know for a fact that's what he was doing.

And he wasn't just watching us, he was *hunting* us."

Chapter 3

Captain Meyers strongly suggested that I sit back down. I didn't want to, but he had his fangs out, and I was feeling more and more like a mouse in the grass, waiting to get struck. He and Triplett stood, stretched, and walked to the door, but didn't leave. They just took turns mumbling in the corner . . . things that I probably should have tried harder to hear. When they finished, Meyers opened the door and asked for somebody to bring us a couple of throw-away cups with ice. My throat was getting dry, I hoped that one of them would be for me.

They sat back down, and Triplett wasted no time. "You mentioned something that happened Saturday that made you think the deer was actually hunting all of you. Tell me about it."

"Saturday morning was actually the best morning of hunting I've ever had. We were all up early, and since the wind was right, I hunted in one of the two stands close to camp. I was sitting in it thirty minutes before daybreak, and at dawn, the whole place erupted . . ."

My mind nearly derailed. It was all I could do to finish the thought. When I said 'at dawn' I had an involuntary shudder right there in the chair, and luckily neither investigator seemed to notice it. Seventeen is too old to be scared of the dark, but I had never really outgrown it. It wasn't the night and darkness that really got to me though, it was that brief time right at dawn that absolutely terrified me. It was that time of the day — at first light — when the grayness and uncertainty that came along with it allowed my eyes to play terrible tricks on me. Limbs weren't just limbs, and brush wasn't just brush. Sometimes they were ghouls, monsters, and other hairy, snarling things poised to pounce on the first poor creature that happened by. With everything that was going on, it seemed silly that I had reacted that way. I suppose everyone has irrational fears, but I sure was glad I didn't have to explain why I shuddered. They already had enough doubts about me, I didn't need to give them any more ammunition.

I swallowed a dry gulp, and continued. "Titmice, chickadees, bluejays, a Cooper's hawk chasing chipmunks, and a raccoon climbed the tree next to mine. You name it, I saw it. I had a good time watching all that, but it was about nine-thirty when I saw her; a pretty doe came meandering by. I noticed her wobbling some, and figured she might have been beat from trying to outrun horny bucks all morning. She stepped into the creek all lathered up and panting, and started to drink. I knew it was going to be an easy shot, and after a second or two to calm down I drew the bow and sent an arrow right through her lungs. She went maybe forty yards and just toppled over. It was my first selfbow kill."

Meyers smirked and said, "Congratulations."

I ignored the sarcastic comment and continued. "I field dressed her in the woods, and once I got her back to camp, I opened her up along her back just enough to take out those two long loins on either side of her spine. It was still cool out, so I figured that I'd finish up the skinning and quartering after lunch. When Al and the others arrived, the charcoal was turning white and I was filleting those back straps on one of the picnic tables under the porch.

They just stood there looking at me for a little bit. Turns out they all had a rotten morning, not seeing anything, and there I was prepping a doe that I'd killed with my homemade wood bow. I gave them a minute to reel their jaws back up before asking them if they were jealous, but nobody answered. I'm not sure what they thought of it, but I was certain about one thing; we were all about to have a fantastic lunch."

Triplett was rubbing both of his temples, thinking, when a deputy opened the door and sat the cups on the desk. Triplett poured his, took a big swallow, and then pointed at the other on the table, and said, be my guest.

It was the best tasting Coke I ever had, and I drained the cup in three pulls. I wiped my mouth and saw that they were both looking at me, waiting. I cleared my throat and said, "Okay, well, being up so early, and after a lunch like that, there was nothing left to do except take a snooze. Sometime later Al got up to make a payment on all that coffee he drank that morning, and on the way to the bathroom he saw something out the big window that didn't register."

"What did he see?"

"The gambrel post had been torn down, and what looked to be a huge buck was dragging that doe carcass across the yard. He thought it was a joke, and he said that he looked around and saw me and Kirby asleep in plain sight, but Renn wasn't. There were a couple of blankets spread out on the couch where Renn had crashed, and Al figured that the lumpy mass under them were just pillows. He said later that he thought that Renn had made it outside without waking anyone and was pulling a prank.

"So Al woke me up rumbling through the living room, and I came to in time to watch him launch himself in the air and land in the middle of the couch. Those lumps weren't pillows after all, and he landed right in the middle of Renn. Renn came boiling from under there with a badly busted nose, hollering . . . it was so bad, we had to use a half a roll of paper-towels to stop the bleeding. While Al was tending to Renn, Kirby and I went outside and checked it out. The gambrel frame was a mess, the doe was gone, and there was an obvious drag mark across the yard leading to the woods. We followed it maybe twenty yards past the woodline, and everything vanished. My doe, whatever Al saw dragging it, and all tracks and sign were simply gone."

Triplett said, "You thought then that maybe it was the folks from the Big Oak club still making trouble?"

"What else could we think?"

"I see what you mean. And after this, you all just decided to go back hunting that evening?"

"It was my first deer with my osage bow, and I only got a few pictures for the magazine and only got a couple of pieces of back-strap out of her. Sure, I was mad, and the others, I think, felt even worse for me, but there was nothing else to do. We weren't going to sacrifice prime hunting to try to get back at the Big Oak guys right away."

Detective Triplett turned a page in his notebook and said, "After all that, you all just laid around for a bit, and then went back hunting that evening. And this is the evening when you first encountered the buck, up close and personal?"

I nodded.

"Tell me about it."

"The other guys went back to the eastern side of the place, where we had seen the big twelve the evening before. I thought about going with them, but decided to try the second stand that Marissa and I set back in December. It was still close to the camp house; maybe a couple of hundred yards away from the stand I shot the doe at that morning. She and I found a funnel where two big oaks had fallen in the woods along the creek. They had been down a while, and basically the vines and brambles had overtaken what was left of them, but there was a small open corridor between them that looked like the boarding zone for the Ark. It was covered in tracks back in December, and I hoped that nothing had changed. I just wanted to kill another deer with my selfbow, and wasn't trying to be too selective. If this spot was still hot, well . . .

"I walked down the small feeder branch, and when I got to where it ran into Indian Mound, I turned left. My stand was just a bit upstream, but before I got there I saw movement. One of those big piles of brambles shook a little, and out steps this big-ass buck. I couldn't see him that well at first, but he started walking my way. He was looking right at me, but apparently he didn't care. He came into the open woods, maybe fifty yards, and I realized who I was looking at."

"It was the twelve pointer?"

"Right. Maybe it was the angle, since I was on the ground with him, but man, that set of antlers looked way bigger than I remembered. But it was him all right — complete with that crazy drop tine. He looked like the king of the forest, with some kind of elaborate self-grown crown. I reached in my quiver and got an arrow on the string, and the quick movement must have set him off. He took a couple of big hops, and in an instant, we were eye to eye at maybe ten steps.

Triplett said, sounding like he didn't believe it, "So the deer didn't run away from you? You think he deliberately came right at you?"

"Crazy huh? It reminded me of those old spaghetti westerns . . . showdown in the street at high noon. There was something going on with him though. At that distance, nothing was hidden. There was definitely something wrong."

"Oh yeah? What was it?"

"It was three things really. Something was all over his neck and chest. A sort of reddish brown crust. It was easy to see on that white hair on his throat. It looked like dried blood. I was close enough to see him blink his eyes, but I couldn't see any cuts or fresh wounds that would make him bleed. And it took just a second or two for me to see that every time he took a breath, he was blowing snot or something out of his nose. Looked like he was sick and his nose was running. And then there were his eyes."

"What was wrong with them?

"I don't know. They just looked darker than normal. Black, nearly. It was like something was in them . . . a film maybe."

Triplett smiled and sat back in his chair. I could tell he didn't believe me. "John, are you sure about all this? Blood but no wounds? Mucous coming out his nose? Black eyes? Aren't a deer's eyes black anyway?

"Haven't you ever seen a deer's eye up close, detective? They are dark, but not jet black. I was close enough to see his eyelashes. This deer's eyes looked like they had been drawn in with a black marker."

I finally had won a small battle. Triplett went silent and pursed his lips, and Meyers looked sheepishly at everything in the room except me. I could feel the corners of my mouth start to rise, but I snuffed the smile and continued. "The buck and I just stared at each other for a bit. I thought about trying to shoot him square in the chest, or maybe right in that rust-stained white throat patch, but I just couldn't do it. That bow of mine is powerful enough to get a broadhead through his sternum, but it would have to be a perfect shot. And the way my arms and hands were shaking, I knew I wouldn't be steady enough to pull it off. I was ready though. If he had charged, I would have shot for sure. Instead, he just stared at me with those crazy black eyes, and after a moment or two, he snorted out a big wad of snot, took off to my right and was gone."

A sick feeling came over me. At that moment, I realized what I had done — or better yet, what I hadn't done. I didn't think about it when I was spilling my guts to Meyers, but I saw it now, as clear as the sky on a bluebird day. I was just ten steps away from this black eyed nightmare, and I didn't shoot. I was rattled and shaking some from being eye to eye with a massive buck, sure, but at that range, I could have hit him somewhere. And even if I hadn't stopped him right there, maybe a bad arrow wound could have kept him from killing the others. It was moot now. I didn't let Meyers or Triplett see, but thinking about it, I almost cried.

Meyers lit another Marlboro, and Triplett looked like he was trying to think of what to say next. He didn't have to say anything . . . his facial expression said it all. He thought I was crazy.

After several moments, Triplett slapped both hands down on the table. "Wait a minute. Wait — just — one — minute." He stood, turned away from the table, and gazed at the smoky haze against the low ceiling. He rocked back and forth on the balls of his feet a few times and said, "Do you mean to tell me that this deer, this, by your definition, lunatic animal, ambushed you in the woods and initiated a staring contest?"

I looked at Captain Meyers and nodded, "That's exactly how it happened, detective."

Still staring at the ceiling, Triplett said, "Captain Meyers, from our conversation earlier about how far a deer might travel across the landscape, I assume you hunt, or at least have a rudimentary understanding of deer behavior?"

Meyers looked a little lost. "I suppose."

"Then please tell me something. Do you believe that a male whitetail deer, crazy or not, sick or not, would come into a camp, knock down the meat pole and drag off a dead, gutted doe — then later on that same day, come boiling out of some thicket and initiate a confrontation with a hunter?"

"I don't think so detective. I've never even read about such nonsense in books."

Triplett turned and sat back down and took a sip of Coke. "Thank you for your opinion Captain." Staring blankly at the generic cup, but talking to me, he said, "John, I feel like I should tell you that I'm having a hard time believing what you are saying, and more importantly implying. But I know there are always situations out in the wild that do not necessarily fall under the big umbrella of *normal* behavior. I do believe there are exceptions to every rule, and I want you to know that I'm not totally considering your account bogus." Triplett's icy blue eyes left the cup and met mine. It was as sincere as I had seen him look yet. "Your story is very interesting, but it's getting to be quite a big pill to swallow. If just one of these aberrations had occurred — just a simple isolated incident — there would be plenty of room for doubt. But this growing list of extraordinary occurrences is becoming more than the benefit of doubt can bear."

I didn't know what he wanted me to say. I had been in the woods all my life, and had never seen anything like it before either. Just because I, Meyers, or Triplett hadn't seen it before doesn't mean that a buck deer couldn't go crazy and kill a few people. Could it?

Chapter 4

Meyers and Triplett took a short break, and walked outside to do whatever detectives do when trying to decode interrogation statements. The room was quiet yet again; my only contentments, if you can call them that, were watching that screwy clock run backwards and listening to my stomach growl. When they returned, right away I could tell that they were in a better mood. Triplett was smiling again, and Meyers — well, at least Meyers wasn't scowling.

The Captain flipped his matchbook around between two fingers and said, "We are going to sneak in one more session before we break for a late lunch, John. The Sheriff wanted me to ask you if you wanted a cheeseburger or something. We've got Jones going by the Burger Barn — he's going to pick up a grab bag of what they call food there. If you wanted something else, tell me now so I can relay the info."

I agreed to whatever they'd bring me, and then Triplett tipped his cup back, belched, and said, "Okay John, after you encountered the big buck, you still hunted that evening. Correct?"

I nodded.

"And I understand that later on in the evening, there were two incidents that occurred. Both were encounters with questionably, or strangely acting animals? A deer and an armadillo. Is that right?"

"Yes"

"Okay, let's talk about it."

"It was hard sitting in the stand that evening. I was still shook up over seeing the big buck, and I just couldn't quite get everything straight in my head. There was a time or two when I thought I was going to hyperventilate, but I remembered a trick dad showed me back when he was teaching me how to hunt — something to calm me down."

"What kind of a trick?" Triplett asked.

"Remember earlier when I told you the story about hearing the buck's antlers ticking on the brush? Well, this was part two of my listening training. One day Dad drug me out in to the woods and actually blindfold me. We sat still for a few minutes, and he asked me what I heard. Well, I heard a bunch of things, but not the things he wanted me to hear. He told me to forget about the big stuff, what I could hear without concentrating, and to focus on what was in the background. After a while, I relaxed and really started to listen. In no time I figured out what he was talking about. Things that weren't there before almost jumped right into my lap: water trickling along in the creek, the light breeze rustling the beech leaves, and a woodpecker scratching up and down the bark of some tree down deeper in the woods. That experience taught me two things that every hunter should know, how to listen, and as a byproduct, how to relax. After being keyed up and face to face with the buck, and maybe worrying about what would happen if I ran into him again, the one thing I needed most was to relax.

"It worked, and I started feeling better just listening to the light breeze, and thrushes and towhees scratching in the leaves behind me. I lost track of time, and even started to doze when I heard footsteps. It sounded like multiple animals, and they were coming my way. I could tell they were going to walk through that opening, so I took a deep breath and opened my eyes. Sure enough, there was a doe and a nice little buck some thirty yards away from me ready to walk, or better yet, stumble through that little opening.

"The doe was acting like the one I shot that morning — panting and swaying and wheezing that clear snot out of her nose. The buck was right behind her and nearly had *his* nose stuck up her rear end. I got an arrow ready and positioned myself to shoot, but they were still a bit far. She took several more steps, staggered, and almost fell. I almost blew it right there; I kept it in but I could have laughed so hard they would've heard me in Halifax. It took them a while, but they finally came through the opening, and I was trying to decide which one to shoot when I noticed the doe's eyes. They looked as black as any eight-ball you've ever seen — just like the big buck's. Before I could draw the bow, the boyfriend must have decided that he wasn't getting enough attention, and he leaned forward and raked his antlers across her flank.

"I know what he was trying to do, but it didn't work. She blew out a hat-full of snot, then she raised her rear leg, blurred something resembling a martial arts maneuver, planting a hoof right between his eyes. He went down hard, but that wasn't enough for her. She bounded backwards, straddled him, and then began pounding with all four hooves. She went on like that for thirty or forty seconds, then as suddenly as it began, it was over. She stood over him, leering, almost taunting him in some savage show of victory, and just when I thought it couldn't get weirder, this crazy doe leaned down and bit a big plug out of this poor buck's neck. That woke him up, because he squealed and got to his feet and limped off bleeding. But this doe, she just stood there staring off into space. I could see blood streaming out of the corners of her mouth."

Triplett, setting the pen down on his note book, said, "This is just getting better and better. Are you sure that's what happened? Or maybe better, is there any way you could have seen it wrong, or interpreted what actually happened incorrectly?"

Meyers shuffled in his seat and squinted at me; one eye almost shut. He wanted to say something, but decided against it at the last second. I knew he wanted to call me a liar.

"I saw what I saw, but that wasn't the worst of it. After a few moments, she actually began chewing. And if that wasn't enough, I watched her swallow. I could hear the big gulp as it went down."

While the two men reeled in their seats, the flashback nearly took my breath away. Watching that doe, a beautiful animal that was supposed to be a gleaming example of grace and pristineness of the natural world, turn into some dirty, conniving mercenary made me sick to my stomach. A hot rage began to build in my guts again, and I gripped the table in front of me with both hands so hard both Meyers and Triplett leaned back. I said, almost sneering, "I had the shot and took it, but the broadhead just clipped some hair off her back, and stuck in the ground behind her. I couldn't believe that I'd missed from that close. She trotted past me, further down the trail, and by the time I settled down and got another arrow ready, she was maybe fifty yards away. Fifty yards, fifty miles — it didn't matter. Anything that acts like that needs to die . . . *deserves* to die. So I drew, estimated the range and aimed as best I could, and let it fly. Just for a moment, I thought I had her, but the distance wasn't right. The arrow fell short, and ten yards further down the trail, the luckiest deer alive, stumbled and fell, gained her feet again, and staggered out of sight."

I cracked my knuckles, trying to calm myself. It was like I stepped out of the stand that quiet evening, and magically appeared in the interrogation room reliving the scene as if it just happened. Taking a deep breath, I locked my fingers together on the table and looked up to see Triplett casually writing in his notebook like it was the Saturday morning grocery list. I turned my head to see Captain Meyers staring at the ceiling, chewing on a fingernail. My hands turned into white-knuckle fists. I ground my teeth wanting to tell them both where they could go and how quick to get there, but I knew there was nothing else I could do or say to make them believe. All I could do was continue with the story.

A few slow breaths later I said, "I know that teenagers don't have much of a reputation for using their heads, but when it comes to life and limb," I tapped my thumb a few times in the middle of my chest, "this teenager is smart enough to know when it's time to *vamoose*. I gave her about five minutes to get out of the neighborhood, and I gathered my stuff and got down and made my way back to camp. I made it to the edge of the yard with about twenty minutes of light to spare, and felt worlds better will all that crap behind me. I stepped out of the woods and *shazam* . . . there was an Andrew Jackson out in the grass between me and the porch?"

Triplett looked bemused. "Andrew who?"

"Andrew Jackson." I gave him a second, then said, "Actually it was an armadillo, but dad hated those little bulldozers so much he offered a standing twenty dollar bounty for every one we could kill."

"Oh, I see."

I put my thumb back to my chest, "This teenager also knows that twenty dollars is twenty dollars. I wasn't about to let a chance to pick up some extra cash slip through my fingers, especially since it looked like this was going to be easy money. When I first saw him, I thought he was dead already. He was on his back with all fours pointing to the sky, but before I got there, he flipped over and started meandering around. I figured that a car might have clipped him and knocked him silly, but as long as he still had a tail, I didn't care."

"How's that?"

"Dad said he'd only pay if we cut the tails off and nail it to the big pine in the backyard. A way of confirming the kill."

Triplett shrugged his shoulders and said, "I guess that would work about as well as anything."

"I walked almost right up to him, and he flipped over one more time, convulsing. When he righted himself, he saw me and stood up on his rear legs, and that's when I shot him through the head with my practice arrow. I picked up my arrow from the grass behind him, wiped it off on my shirt-tail, slid it back in my quiver and then cut his tail off and went to the camp house for the hammer and nails."

Triplett scribbled something in his notebook and asked, "And that is how you claim the arrow and your shirt got blood on them, huh? By shooting a twenty dollar bill right through the head?"

This time, I shrugged *my* shoulders. "That's what happened."

What I didn't bother to tell Meyers and Triplett, was that after I nailed that tail to the pine, washed up and started on supper, I had plenty of time to really think about what happened. It didn't seem that scary while it was happening, but if the situation had been just a little different, I could have been the one being pounded by sharp hooves and getting a plug of meat bitten from my neck. I sat there at the picnic table and almost unraveled. The only thing that kept me from falling completely apart were three questions that kept racing around in my head. Why had they acted so screwy? Why did their eyes look so black? And what was the deal with all that snot?

The reality is that I'm no closer to answering those questions now, than I was there at camp that evening right after it happened. There were no answers then, and there aren't any now.

It had been a strange day up to that point, but what I saw so far was just a light appetizer compared to the main course that was still yet to come.

Chapter 5

That evening was actually quite lovely. The light breeze danced with the long pine needles hanging in the trees, and it was just cool enough for a jacket. The picnic table on the porch stood sentinel over its simple world, while the wounded Webber streamed a steady column of sweet smelling meat smoke into the cool night air. A Barred owl hooted in the distance while the full moon started climbing through the bare trees to the east, shining down its pale, pearly light in broken small shafts across the yard. The sky couldn't look this pretty in St. Louis. The steaks sizzled loudly, and the orange light from the flare-up shone through the cracked air vents of the grill kettle. I flipped the steaks again and looked my watch, counting the minutes. The guys were late — something had happened . . .

The memory faded, and I was back in the interrogation room just in time to hear Triplett ask me for the second time what happened after the armadillo. I shuttered in my seat thinking about it, and this time both investigators noticed.

"What's wrong John?" Triplett asked.

"Sorry. An honest reaction, I guess."

"Reaction to what?"

"What you just asked about. Al, Renn, Kirby — they were all killed. That's what happened next."

"I understand this might be a bit traumatic for you. Captain Meyers told me that you broke down before with this part of your statement. It's probably going to hurt a little, but I really need to hear exactly what you saw when those men died. Take a deep breath, and just go at whatever pace you're comfortable with."

I closed my eyes, tried to swallow, and began reliving the worst hour of my life. "Thirty minutes after they should have been back, Al pulled up to the porch and told me that supper was going to have to wait. Kirby saw the big twelve and got off a shot at him. They needed all the light and eyes they could get to help track him. I made a face at Al. He saw it and laughed."

Triplett didn't understand, so I tried to explain. "Detective, Kirby McNeil was what some folks would call an embellisher. The rest of humanity would call him something worse. When things were dull around camp, he sort of fabricated fantastic stories to amuse himself and the rest of us. He told them for the truth, but most of the time they were so far-fetched, you simply couldn't believe any part of them. After a while, you just wrote off everything he said. You remember me telling you that he wasn't my favorite person? Well, now you know why."

Triplett's his upper lip twitched a couple of times. I knew what he was thinking.

"So we are all down in the woods near the creek standing around a spot of dark red blood and a pinch of white hair. Kirby told his side of the story, and it sounded an awful a lot like the story we all had from Friday evening. He said the buck somehow spotted him, but when he was maneuvering to try to get a shot, the stand creaked and the deer jetted. But before he got out of sight, he stopped and looked back at him one last time. The deer was partly hidden in a tangle of branches, but there was a small opening he could easily see through leading right to the deer's midsection. Kirby said he didn't shoot a .300 Magnum for nothing, and quickly lined it up and squeezed off a shot.

"Well, he and Renn nearly got into a fist fight right there. Renn was pissed at him for not being patient and waiting for another chance and a better shot. Kirby's rebuttal was that it was only a hundred and twenty-five yards, and the opening was as big as a basketball, and he knew he had the shot, or he *would* have waited. They went back and forth a few times, and Kirby tried to blame the whole she-bang on the deer stand for creaking. He may have made everything else up, but he was right about those stands. We bought a few last summer from a small start-up company in Birmingham, but apparently they hadn't worked all the kinks out of their prototypes. If the wind blew or if you shifted weight in them, those things squeaked like a rusty hinge in a horror movie.

"So Renn and Kirby were about to tie up when Al finally stepped in and separated the two. He looked at Kirby and told him to take a deep breath and tell him more about the shot. There wasn't much more to tell, and we all agreed to channel our energy into taking up the trail. We tracked it as best we could, probably for sixty yards. There wasn't a whole lot of blood to begin with, but after we covered that distance, it was like turning off a dripping spigot. We gathered around the last speck of it, and poor Kirby was almost crying.

"He knew as well as we did that we weren't going to find the deer. I didn't want to say it out loud, but the sparse dark blood and the white hair most likely meant that the bullet had probably just nicked him on his belly

— hardly a fatal wound. I actually started to feel sorry for Kirby, and I think Al was thinking the same thing. He slapped him on the back and said that it didn't look good, but we were going to give it one last chance. He took off his orange hat and hooked it on a limb, marking the spot, and told everyone to fan out and start making small search circles.

"We probably did that for two minutes, and then it happened. I was on my hands and knees with my flashlight looking for specks of blood, and to my left there was a rush of wind, a big thud, and Renn screaming. I got to my feet in a hurry, and heard the awfullest commotion I've ever heard. It was like he was being dragged through the woods by a car on the end of a rope. Then it stopped somewhere down the creek bottom. But it just didn't fade away, like it was the distance that kept me from hearing it. No, Renn's screaming stopped abruptly, like he ran into something. I shined my light around and Al and Kirby stood about twenty steps from me staring off into the woods in the direction of the screams. Their mouths were open like mine.

"We huddled up, all asking the same question, 'What the hell was that?' We were all scared, but didn't know anything else to do but to try to see what happened. So we walked to Renn's flashlight laying in the leaves, and we saw the line of chewed up ground. We followed it, and I quickly noticed that Al had a revolver in his hand. Considering what we thought just happened, I felt a little better knowing that at least one of us had a gun. After maybe fifty yards or so, whatever it was came at us again. It whooshed by me, hit Kirby center mass, and took him with it. Al and I wheeled on our heels, and our lights caught the tail end of it before it got out of sight. It was large and brown and looked like a deer's haunch, and above it we could see Kirby floating in the air and screaming. That image froze in my mind as it lunged out of sight.

"It was so weird. I know I saw a deer's rear end, and Kirby pegged on the antlers above it, but my brain just couldn't accept it. It was like my regular scheduled thoughts were interrupted by a public service announcement, 'Excuse me ladies and gentlemen, regular programming will resume shortly, but the good folks from your cerebellum want you to know that what you just saw was a hoax. I repeat, do not believe what you just saw.'

"I don't know how long it took, but after studying the image that wasn't real, and remembering what I heard when Renn disappeared, I called bullshit on the public service announcement. There was no other explanation. Renn and Kirby were attacked by a huge buck."

Meyers grunted and huffed another smoke ring into the air.

I tried to ignore him, "I was so shocked I couldn't say anything, and Al was standing beside me stuttering. He finally blurted out something about getting the hell out of there, and he frantically turned a circle, asking which way was the truck. Well, with all the tracking and turning around, I wasn't too sure which way to go either. I can still hear him saying, 'Jesus Johnny! We can't just leave them down here, but we aren't doing them or ourselves much good just walking around in circles waiting for whatever that thing was to come back and have a go at us.' There was a second or two of quiet, then he cocked his head and pointed. I heard it too. The creek was to our left, and the truck was downstream.

"The last thing Albert Rutledge said was, 'If we can just get to the creek, we should be able to find . . .' Then it was like the night just opened up and gave birth to a fur covered demon. It was maybe five steps from us when I first saw it, but I don't think Al ever saw it until it was on him. I could see the pistol flying through the air, and I could hear bones popping and what sounded like his lungs bursting."

I stopped for a second, and shuttered in my chair again. I looked up at Meyers and Triplett, two blurry masses behind a wall of tears. I still couldn't believe it. How could it have happened? What made him do it? It was the most savage thing I'd ever seen!

Triplett stood, and walked over to me. He put his hand on my shoulder and asked if I was okay. I wiped my eyes on the backs of my hands and nodded. He suggested that we take a break, but I shook my head. I was nearly through with the worst of it, and I wanted to get it over with. I motioned towards his chair, and without saying anything, he seemed to understand. He sat back down, picked up the pen, and turned a concerned face to Meyers.

"I just stood there helplessly watching the deer push him along the ground, goring and goring — God it was brutal! Then the deer raised his head, lifting his bloody prize off the ground. Al was still conscious and fighting, trying to get off the antlers, but it was no use. The more he struggled, the deeper he sank. I could hear him gurgling, and then he went limp. The deer finally bolted and rammed Al against —"

There was a knock on the door. One of the deputies stuck his head inside and said, "Sorry to interrupt sirs. Sheriff wanted me to tell you that lunch is here."

Meyers motioned angrily at him and said, "Okay Jones, we'll be through here in a few minutes. Tell the Sheriff to keep his pants on."

The door closed and they both turned to me again. They looked like children expecting a fantastic ending to a book their teacher was reading to them in class.

Triplett said, "Sorry about that John. You were saying . . . Al was what? About to be rammed against something?"

I closed my eyes, reliving that final horrible moment. "I still can't believe it. That deer took a couple of big hops, and rammed Al square into the butt of a big tree. He did it again, and then for a third time. That last one is what finished him off. When he hit, I know I heard Al's spine snap."

Chapter 6

I was escorted back to the holding cell, and the burger, fries, and drink were sitting on the cot. After reliving the massacre, I really didn't feel like eating. I nibbled at the cheeseburger, and downed a fry or two, and noticed that the phone was ringing constantly up the hall. Sometimes I could hear parts of conversations, depending on how close to their doors the Sheriff and Meyers were when they were speaking. I quickly realized that Al, Renn, and Kirby's families were taking turns calling, asking if there had been any new developments. My heart sank again. I hadn't even considered what their families must be going through. Then I thought of mom and dad. Meyers told me earlier on that they had been notified, but I hadn't been able to talk with them yet. Whenever that happened, history would be made — the scariest phone call in the history of man.

A few minutes later, a deputy walked by and saw that I was just picking at the cheeseburger. He asked me if I wanted something else to eat, but I just shook my head. Every time I closed my eyes, the only thing I could see was Al hanging on those antlers.

***

After lunch the same deputy walked me back to the empty interrogation room, and a few minutes later, the investigators walked back in.

Triplett turned to a new page in the notebook and said, "Now that the tough part is over, John, I think we can speed up some. Let's move right along if you don't mind. There are still a few things that we need to talk about it depth, but most of what's left I think we can breeze right over it. Whatta you say?"

"Whatever you want is fine by me."

"Okay then. One of the things I really need to get straight is how you escaped. We probably need to spend a little time there. I'm ready whenever you are."

"Well, after watching what happened, I couldn't move. The buck turned and looked right at me, and there was Al, still hanging lifeless above his head. The deer bowed and swept his head side to side along the ground, trying to dislodge his bloody payload. Then it dawned on me that I was next. There was no time to think, I did the only thing I could do . . . I ran. I went as far as I could as fast as I could, but slowly, the electricity running through my legs started to fade, and so did my speed. As I slowed, I looked at the water in the creek, and realized that I was running the wrong way. Upstream. I didn't want to turn around and head back towards ground zero, and really I was just happy to have put a little distance between me and the buck while he was busy trying to get Al off his antlers. I managed a little breathing room, but I had a feeling it wouldn't last.

"I've had been on that part of the creek a bunch coon hunting with my friend Darrell from high school, but running through those woods, nothing looked familiar. Everything was just a wooded blur at the end of the flashlight beam. I stopped for just a moment to catch my breath, and I thought of the twin tangles where I saw the buck earlier. It was still a good ways up the creek, but there was no way I could miss that little passage between the two tangles. If I got that far, my stand was right there and at least I could get off the ground. And if for some reason the deer didn't follow me, instead of climbing, I could go on out to the camp house. It was a no-brainer, so I started running and dodging trees."

Triplett stopped me. "So you ran up the creek instead of down the creek." He flipped a couple of pages in the notebook. And the truck was downstream . . . right?"

I nodded.

"I assume the truck would have been the best defense in your situation. Why didn't you try to run in a big circle, effectively double-backing, to try to get back to it?"

"The creek was my compass. As long as I could see it, I knew about where I was. Trusting myself to pull a big loop with no landmarks and keep on track in the dark wasn't going to happen."

Weren't there stands positioned along the creek in the food plots you all have? Why didn't you try for one of those, instead of deciding to go all the way up the creek?"

"I thought about that for a second or two, but we all hang our own stands, and even though I had an idea where some would be, but that wouldn't be good enough in the dark. We all sort of tell each other where we are hunting, and sometimes we get specific with where we put our stands, but if you haven't walked right to them, you still have to search them out. I felt like I didn't have a lot of extra time to do that. But I knew exactly where my stand was up the creek."

Triplett, apparently satisfied with my explanation, asked me to continue.

"I made it probably another couple of hundred yards with a few briers ripping at me before I tripped over a root or something. I went down hard and my flashlight slipped and went into the air." I shook my head still thinking about how improbable it was. "I could have done that a hundred times and it not land the same way again."

"What happened?"

"The dang thing hit the ground probably eight or ten feet in front of me, shining right back at my face. I caught two retinas full of blinding white light with ultra-dilated pupils. I got to my feet, gulping air, unable to see, and not knowing what to do. I wanted to scream, but something told me not to. Then I remembered what dad said, 'There will be times when your eyes will be useless.' Boy was he ever right!

"My eyes were still trying to adjust, so I stood still for another moment, listening. There was an owl and a few other night birds doing their thing, and I could hear the creek flowing, but back behind me, there was a low rumble. Every second, it got louder and louder. I knew he was coming for me.

"Another shot of adrenaline hit. I grabbed the flashlight, but before I could get going, I heard something strange. I stopped for a second and then realized what it was. The wind was blowing some, and somewhere up ahead one of those cheap stands was squeaking. It might as well been a singing choir of angels! As psychotic as that deer was, there was no way he could climb a tree. So, I ran towards where I heard it, but knew that it would take another gust of wind, and a lucky sweep of the light to find it."

Detective Triplett interrupted again. "Why did you need the stand? You said yourself that the deer couldn't climb, yet, how many trees did you run by during this sprint?

"Most of the timber on the Rutledge property, especially along Indian Mound, is all mature hardwoods. They're all big around as fifty-five gallon drums, and there's not a limb on them for a while. I'm not a monkey; there's no way to climb trees that big and expect to make it thirty or forty feet up before getting to a limb. No, I had to have something I could climb easily. Screw-in steps, or a ladder from a deer stand was my only hope.

"So I was running towards where I thought I heard the squeak, when I felt the cool wind on my face. The wind was going again, and I crossed everything I could cross, hoping and praying that I'd hear it again. And out in front of me there was a long, almost pulsing *creeeaaakkk!!!*"

"And how far was the deer from you when you heard it?

"I don't know . . . close. I didn't waste time checking. By the time I saw that screw-in step shine on the side of the tree, it felt like he was in my hip pocket. I took the light between my teeth and started climbing. I had just cleared the fourth step when he hit the tree below me. I covered the rest of the steps in record time and got on the platform and looked down. The buck was down there staggering and shaking his head — the bark where he hit the tree was shredded. It was as close as close gets. If I'd been a second or two slower, he'd have tossed me on those antlers like a human salad. He circled the tree a couple of times, and was breathing hard from all the running, but it sounded screwed up, almost bubbling, blowing snot everywhere. When he finally caught his breath, he reared up on the tree like a coon dog, and looked up at me with those two crazy black eyes. I halfway expected him to bark."

Meyers smirked and chucked as Triplett said, "And that is where you sat all night? In that deer stand?"

I nodded.

"And how long did the deer stay under you?" He shuffled through several pages in Meyers' notes, stopped and read something. He pointed to his watch and said, "And don't tell me you don't know, because I know you were wearing your watch."

I shrugged my shoulders and said, "He was there until three o'clock. That was the last time I checked before I nodded off. I woke up about thirty minutes before dawn, and he was gone."

"You actually went to sleep in a deer stand after all that?"

"Sure, I was exhausted for one, and I knew I was safe as long as I didn't fall out."

"What made you think you wouldn't fall out?"

"I used the small rope attached to the stand. We use them to pull up our guns, bows, and other gear. I put my back against the tree, wrapped myself up good at the midsection, and tied a healthy knot."

"And what woke you up so early? Was the stand uncomfortable?"

I shook my head and said, "Nightmares."

Chapter 7

The detective was right. The stand was uncomfortable, but I would have traded every last ounce of whatever comfort there was to rid myself of those horrible nightmares. They were like something straight out of a Stephen King novel. Most of them involved spooky sets of free-floating antlers chasing us through the woods. We'd run, but always would trip, and then the antlers would gore and gore until we were on the verge of drifting off in to that final blackness. Then, in what seemed an act of insulting dominance, we were suddenly freed, and the chase began all over again. When I woke up that last time, the images of the guys still hanging from antlers lingered in my conscious mind for a few moments too long. My stomach knotted, and I leaned over the edge of the stand and vomited.

As bad as I felt waking up in the dark, drenched with sweat and wondering if I was still alive or not, it wasn't as bad as the looks Captain Meyers, and Detective Triplett had on their faces. In the silence, with only Meyers' Timex still cheerfully ticking off the seconds, Triplett read, then wrote, read, then wrote in that little moleskine notebook. His body language was flat, his expression, cold and distant, and somewhere in my mind I thought I could actually hear what he was thinking. He thought that I was a very good story-teller, but the story I was telling was explicit fantasy. The way he flipped back and forth between his notes and Meyers', he had to be double-checking my delivery, the content, and possibly even the timing against the ones I'd given Meyers earlier. He expected to find a discrepancy, maybe something I made up along the way to cover new questions, but it's easy to tell a story that actually happened the same way every time.

I could see one more thing written all over the detective's face. Impatience. He had insisted on informality, allowed me to talk some about how I hunted, given me as much leeway and time he could while I was telling my side of things, and he still hadn't received the pay-off. I didn't know exactly what he was expecting to find, but he remained cordial, even after I boldly defended myself on a couple of bad questions. He was still trying to dig something out of me.

Meyers was much easier to read. He just sat in his chair watching us talk. When his chin wasn't propped in his hand, he was perfecting smoke rings between yawns.

Triplett finished writing and said, "So tell me something, John. There's a part of this that I'm not following. Going back over your statements you say you encountered five deer all together. There was the buck you, Albert, and Renfro saw the first night, then there was the doe you killed Friday evening."

"Yes sir. That's the one that Al saw the buck drag off right after lunch."

"Right. Then there was the big buck that you had the staring contest with when walking to your stand early Saturday evening."

"It had to be the same deer. The one we all saw Friday evening. The one Al saw drag my doe off, and the one that jumped out of the bushes at me early Saturday evening . . . it had to be him."

"Okay" the detective said, running the tip of his pen along lines in the notebook. "Then Saturday evening, after the staring contest, you saw two deer. A doe and a buck. This one was a different buck, right? You called him a 'nice little buck.' He wasn't the twelve pointer with the drop tine? And the doe, you indicated, seemed a little off — drunk maybe. You said that she seemed to be walking funny. And of course there were the strange reactions to the buck when he gave her a little love tap. All that seems contrary to how deer normally act, doesn't it?"

I nodded again.

"But what about that smaller buck? You said when they approached, it sounded like they both were walking sort of funny. But from the actions you described, he seemed like he was normal. Did he, or didn't he look drunk? Or maybe he was just walking funny from an eager pecker? Did you see his eyes? Did they look black like the other ones that clearly were acting funny?"

The pressure was staring to build. Triplett was now showering me with tough questions, and he was asking them forcefully, like he was trying to steer me into a trap. I thought about what happened, and then trying to stay calm, I took a full breath and said, "I don't know. I don't think he was acting funny. I do know he wasn't blowing snot like the doe. And after she bit him, he ran pretty straight and solid, or as well as he could with a chunk of neck missing."

Triplett's eyes went across the pages of his notebook like a hungry Red-tailed hawk scanning a meadow for a rabbit. When he finished reading, he looked at Captain

Meyers, then back over at me. "Why was this deer okay while all the others you saw seemed to be impaired?"

I shrugged my shoulders. "I don't know if he was fine or not. It all happened so quickly. I didn't really pay much attention to him after he got Bruce Lee-ed."

The detective thumbed back a couple of pages. "You said he raked her flank with an antler." He turned to the resident deer expert and asked, "Is this normal behavior, Captain?"

Meyers exhaled a cloud of smoke and said, "I don't know if I've ever seen a buck do that, but I've heard about them laying their ears back and nipping at each other like horses do. And I've seen them rear up on their back legs and flail at each other with their hooves. Then there's the antler fighting bucks do this time of year. When it comes time to mate, I think they can be as aggressive and peculiar as we are."

"Okay, so let's say the buck was just giving her a playful nudge to let her know he was in the mood. I know it's just a judgment call, but I think for the moment we can call that normal behavior. And then the doe reacts the way she did — in other words — abnormal behavior. That's the part I'm not following. The buck seemed fine, but the doe wasn't. Both animals presumably were coming from the same direction, and should have been exposed to a very similar, if not identical environment prior to appearing."

At that moment, the kinder, gentler Detective Triplett changed. He looked almost triumphant, like he'd just won a high school debate. He leaned back into his chair, interlocking fingers behind his head, and sighed. "Now that's mighty interesting. I'm not quite sure of the implications just yet, but if you think about it, you've told us about several deer sightings in a twenty-four hour period from Friday evening through Saturday evening. Of all the deer that were seen at camp by you, Al, Renfro, and Kirby, you saw every single one of them at some point in time. And only *one* deer out of the lot of them seemed to be normal, or at least not psychotic, or deranged, or whatever you want to call it." Triplett suddenly came forward, I could feel his eyes jabbing holes in me like sharp icepicks. "You're right, it doesn't make sense. You are telling us this wild story, and you don't understand it yourself. How do you think we feel? Do you realize how this makes you look?"

I couldn't answer him. I stared at the ceiling for a minute, trying to decide what would be the safest thing to say. Nothing came to me, so I tried to stall. "I told you at the beginning of all this I didn't think I was going to be much help. It probably would have saved us all a good bit of time if you and the Captain just went for an early lunch, and you two could have read and re-read my previous statements from the Captain's notes and drawn whatever conclusions you wanted to from them."

They didn't respond, and in the momentary silence my mind shifted into gear. I pointed to Meyers, "Just like the Captain said before you came in — he didn't think I could tell it the same way three times in a row. And all the stuff we're doing now is y'all trying to catch me screwing the story up so you can call me a liar. Well, I'm almost done with it for the third time — how am I doing so far? It should be lining up pretty well. Is it?"

Just as Triplett opened his mouth, the rest of what I wanted to say finally lined up in my brain. "Wait a minute, detective. I've got something else to say. With all this talk of deer and deer behavior, especially this time of the year, I think I have an idea of why that last buck seemed okay. You know the rut is going on, right? Well, back when you were in high school or maybe even college and you were rutting, weren't drunk chicks easier to hit on than sober ones? That buck might have thought the same thing. Heck, even I've been to enough parties to know that drunk chicks are the quickest to come out of their clothes."

That finally did it. I could see both Triplett's and Meyers' faces turning red. A big blue vein popped out on the Captain's forehead and pulsed visibly like a metronome. I knew that I was tip-toeing down the line drawn in the sand, but the way things were shaping up, that was just as good of an answer as any. Were they going to sit there and tell me that couldn't have happened? Who's to say that rutting bucks don't look for easy scores? As far as we all knew, that might very well be first chapter material in the 'Whitetail Deer Dating and Sex Guide' book, and fall comfortably under Triplett's wonderfully wide umbrella of normal deer behavior.

Triplett looked ready to explode, but after a few tense moments, he rolled his head around a couple of times, released a long breath, and smiled. "You've got to understand our position here, John. You've given us practically nothing to go on. We have three out of four men in a hunting party dead. We have you, the only survivor, having access to all the areas where everyone was murdered. We have you knowing almost exactly where all three bodies were, or at least very close. We have blood on your shirt and on one of your arrows, and by the way, that arrow, which had your fingerprints all over it, matches the wound channels on all three victims perfectly. We've just sat through a fantastically imaginative tale where you claim the very animals you were hunting somehow morphed into hunters themselves, and finally into carnivorous man-killers. And just for the record, after I got the call from Sheriff Butters and realized that this might be connected with a loopy deer, I took the liberty to check with the state game folks in Montgomery, Atlanta, and Jackson, and with the research professors in the natural resource departments at Auburn, Mississippi State, and UGA just in case. There have been no instances in recorded history where a deer, let alone several, have gone rouge, and decided to start hunting hunters or humans in general. No disease or genetic mutation that we know of has ever rendered a deer aggressive to humans, to the point of them hunting and seeking to kill."

I could see Captain Meyers out of the corner of my eye. He was nodding his head and smiling. Triplett hadn't come right out and said it, but he effectively had just called me a liar, in his kinder and gentler way. Meyers was enjoying it, and before Triplett or I could say anything else, he leaned forward and pointed at my practice arrow still sealed in the plastic evidence bag.

"We know you said the blood on this arrow shaft was from the armadillo you shot in the camp yard. Well, we took it to the forensics lab over at Auburn yesterday afternoon. Our fax machine down the hall is waiting for the results to come in, and when it lights up, I can't wait to hear the story you're going to fabricate that explains how an armadillo came to have human blood in it. Blood that in all likelihood will match at least one of the victims . . . and if we swabbed it down well enough, maybe all three."

Chapter 8

I suppose I couldn't blame them for thinking what they were thinking. Triplett's splendid unrehearsed oratory could have been used as the closing argument for the prosecution at my trial. Of course the blood wasn't going to match, but that probably wouldn't matter. I'm sure they would say that I shot the armadillo after I killed my three companions. Unless I could somehow make sense out of all this, and be able to get them to understand and believe, it was becoming more and more apparent that it was going to take some outside help to clear me. It was a terrible thought, but what I really needed was for something to happen down there again while I was sitting here talking to the investigators. I didn't want anyone else to die, but there was no way they could ignore a glaring alibi like that.

"Just a few more things, John," Triplett said with a labored voice. "With all this death and destruction, would you mind telling me how you managed to get out of the woods in one piece?"

I wanted to drag him through all the crazy schizophrenic episodes that I suffered through when I realized that the deer could be waiting for me behind every tree. I wanted him to feel how scared I was. I wanted him to run through the same woods I ran through, and to experience a mind so absorbed with horror that it could barely function at all.

It wasn't happening though. I couldn't make myself go down that dark alleyway again, so I saved both of us the trouble.

"When dawn came, the deer was gone, and I spent a couple of hours just looking and listening. At first I thought that the deer not being there was a good thing, but then I realized that not knowing which clump of brush he was hiding behind between me and the truck was absolutely frightening. For those two hours, I thought I saw him a thousand times in a thousand places, but it was just my eyes playing tricks on me. You know, I actually considered just sitting in the stand until we were missed and somebody came looking for us. But nobody expected us back until Thursday, and there was no telling how long mom and dad were going to be in St. Louis. Three or four or more days in a deer stand without food or water wasn't going to happen. Eventually I worked up the nerve to climb down."

I stopped for a moment to think. I couldn't decide whether to tell them that by that time, I was staring to doubt it all myself. Truth be known, I had some really interesting arguments with the voices in my head over whether I had dreamed all this up, or if what I saw happen actually happened. The evidence was there. The leaves were parted, leaving a circular trail around the tree, the scarred place on the tree where the antlers hit was dripping sap, and I even kneeled and rubbed the slick remnants of a snot ball between my fingers.

Maybe I was convinced — maybe not. There was one thing that would settle the argument for good.

Al.

I looked at Meyers, then back to Triplett, "I needed to go back to Al's body. I needed to find that .357. At least then I could defend myself just in case that big son of a gun came at me again. I slowly worked my way downstream, looking for anything, but didn't see so much as a red bird. I spotted Al's orange hat hanging in the limb, and there was the plowed up trail where Renn had been pushed along the ground, and then I saw him."

"The deer or one of the bodies?"

"Al. He was laying in the leaves face up, eyes and mouth open like he died screaming. He was covered in blood, his jacket was shredded, and I could see several holes in his chest where the tines got him. I said a quick prayer, and then thought about finding Renn and Kirby, but all the moving and running when it all happened — I couldn't remember exactly where they'd be. There was nothing I could do for them anyway, except make it out alive, and truthfully, I didn't want to spend a lot of time searching for bodies anyway. The revolver was what I needed, so that's what I concentrated on. I moved to where I thought we were standing when the deer hit him. I could see it all happen so vividly, I could almost count the rotations that Ruger made flying through the air. I looked and looked, but it just wasn't there, and I started to get nervous — like I could feel something watching me. I quickly decided that my time would be better spent headed for the truck, so I left."

"Meyers' notes say you didn't go to the truck, you went back upstream all the way to the camp house. Why did you do that?"

"I hadn't gone fifty yards, and I got to thinking. If I was that buck, and I was dead set on killing me, where would be the likeliest place I'd go."

Flatly, Triplett said, "The truck."

"Right. I figured that if ole bucky was waiting to ambush me at the truck, he was going to have to wait a mighty long time. I did an about face, and hauled my rear end up Indian Mound all the way back to camp."

"And you didn't encounter any other deer while doing that?"

"Strange, but no. Every step I took felt scarier than the last, but I didn't notice much of anything on the way through there. The woods were about as dead as I've ever seen them."

Detective Triplett had finally heard enough. "Well, John, that just about does it." He picked up Meyers' notepad off the table, and examined a couple of pages. "The rest of it sounds pretty simple. It says here that when you got back to camp, you picked up a few things, including your bow and arrows, and struck out on the county road headed towards State Highway 223. Once on the highway, you ran or jogged or walked north towards Halifax for an hour before Mr. Weston Peebles picked you up and brought you in."

I nodded.

"Are you absolutely sure you didn't see anything of the buck or any other deer for that matter while you were either getting out of the woods, or making your way north on the road?"

"No sir, I didn't."

"Mr. Peebles told the deputies that you waved him down, and was nearly hysterical, asking him for a ride to

Halifax . . . to the Sheriff's office. When he asked you what was wrong, you said that you needed to report a crime, but you didn't tell him what it was." The detective's eyes moved slowly from the paper to me. "Why didn't you tell him what happened?"

"I figured he wouldn't believe me."

"And you thought we'd believe a story like this?"

"No, but what else was I going to do? I had to tell the authorities, and that's you. At least you'd be able to investigate. You could go and look at the bodies, and look at those piles of snot, and maybe find the deer."

"It says here the bodies were recovered that afternoon, a few hours before nightfall. You lead the recovery party to Albert's body, and that Renfro's and Kirby's bodies were recovered close by. No deer were seen during the recovery, and the scar on the tree you allegedly spent the night in was documented, and there were deer tracks around, but there were no mucous or snot balls found where you said they would be, or anywhere else they looked."

"I don't know what happened to that stuff, maybe they just soaked into the ground or something?"

"The Ruger revolver, a GP-100 model chambered in .357 magnum, was recovered in the leaves approximately thirty-five feet from Albert's body. The cylinder was full and no shots had been fired from it recently. Your finger prints were not found on it, only Albert's." Triplett closed his eyes and pinched the bridge of his nose. "This wasn't a shock to us though. The wounds found on the bodies were puncture wounds, not gunshots — and of course we've already discussed the particulars of your bloody arrow."

Before anything else was said, a deputy appeared at the narrow door. He looked as if somebody had just punched him in the guts. He motioned both investigators over, and I couldn't hear what they were whispering, but a lot of information was being transferred. Detective Triplett turned back to me and asked me to sit tight, and all three men walked out of the room. On the way out I heard Captain Meyers say in a low voice, "You've got to be kidding me!"

Part III

Chapter 1

John Bateman sat alone again in the little interrogation room with nothing to do but twiddle his thumbs. The wall clock was still running backwards, so the idea of time was just a dream. He stared at it for three negative minutes, before he sighed and stood and walked to the mirror. Cupping hands to his face, he leaned forward and peered into and through his own image.

The door suddenly blew open, and Triplett and Meyers walked back in. Meyers was holding a stack of new papers and seemed amused from the start they gave John. "Gotta stay on your toes around here." He pointed towards the mirror and asked, "Trying to figure it out?"

"Nah, just bored."

Meyers smile melted, and he and Triplett sat down while John stared back into the mirror. Triplett looked at his watch, and said, "Before we go any further, I want you to know this will be our final session today. It's going on four o'clock, and I still have a couple of hours of work to do when I get back to Montgomery. I've got court in the morning, but will be out by lunch, hopefully sooner. Whatever we don't cover in the next thirty minutes or so, we'll just pick up on tomorrow afternoon. Are we all on the same page here?"

There was no argument.

"Okay, then. Well, it looks like foul play or some kind of a set-up or frame job from the members of the Big Oak

Hunt Club can be been ruled out. None of their members were hunting Friday or Saturday, and their alibis check out."

John shrugged his shoulders as he walked back to the table. "Okay."

Triplett shuffled through the papers in his hands, finding the one he was looking for. "Also, we got word from the lab over at Auburn. Looks like you were telling the truth about the blood we found on the arrow and your shirt tail. Results show that it was armadillo blood, but the lab also indicated that there was a trace amount of something else in it. A chemical called . . ."

Detective Triplett tried, but couldn't pronounce it. He ran his finger along the bottom of the word printed on the paper while spelling it out loud.

"Z-O-L-P-I-D-E-M"

John looked puzzled. He pronounced the big word perfectly, then said, "Isn't that the chemical name for Bipferin?"

Both investigators' eyes swelled.

"That's right," Captain Meyers said, raising a freshly lit cigarette to his lips. "Now would you mind telling us exactly how you knew that? And anything else you might know about this drug for that matter?"

"I don't know much about it, but I've heard dad talk about it some. It's a drug his company handles distribution for here in the southeast. He is lead rep for Gulf Pharmaceuticals in this region — remember?"

Meyers looked annoyed. "Yeah sure. I remember. Now what's the significance? What does this mean to you and me right now?"

"You live with a drug rep, you hear things. Hear them enough and it sticks. Bipferin is a trade name for zolpidem, and it's supposed to be all the rage these days. I think people use it for a sleep aid, or for relaxation. You know, mellowing out. Dad calls it a pint of bourbon in a pill."

John could see it in their faces. It was one more strike against him. So it wasn't just a straight murder case at the hands of a psycho teenager after all — the presence of a drug in the equation solidified the idea that he could have been under the influence at hunting camp.

The detective turned another page in his notebook and scribbled notes. As he wrote, he asked, "So, is this stuff a narcotic?"

John stared blankly at his hands on the table. "I really don't know."

Still writing, Triplett asked, "How do you think traces of this got into an armadillo's bloodstream in Nowhereville Jessup County? There's no such thing as a natural source of this stuff is there?"

"I believe it's a synthetic drug, but I don't know for sure. I can't say whether a form of it exists naturally or not. How it got into an armadillo? Your guess is as good as mine. I can tell you this though, dad is mighty tight with the samples of everything he gets. He's old school. You know, he keeps up with everything himself — pen and pad. I've seen his inventory forms; I think even the dust on those bottles is accounted for. If you don't believe me, Captain Meyers or anyone else around here that knows him will tell you the same thing. He kept up with that stuff like he runs hunting camp. I can't imagine it happening, but I suppose somebody could have stolen from dad's samples, but I think it would be easier to steal it from a drugstore."

There was a brief moment of silence, then John asked the question that seemed to be on the tip of everyone's tongues: "It doesn't make sense. If you go to the trouble to lift some Bipferin, why would you waste it on an armadillo?"

Both investigators considered the question, staring at John as if to say, *I don't know son. Why don't you tell us the answer to that one*?

A moment later, Meyers touched Triplett on the shoulder. "Detective Triplett, would you please step outside with me?"

Both men left the room, and after a few minutes, they came back through the narrow door.

The detective cleared his throat and said, "You brought up an interesting point while ago. You indicated that it was unlikely, but still possible that some of your dad's stuff could have been taken. If it's possible, then the obvious solution would be somebody that knew his habits and schedule. A person with intimate knowledge of what he does and where he goes — you know — his routine. Is that somebody you, John? Did you slip some of your dad's samples?"

John was shaking his head, but before he could answer, Meyers forcefully said, "What we are trying to tell you is that if you did take some of this stuff, and got bombed out of your skull, the charges against you would be greatly reduced. Second degree murder, negligent homicide, possibly even a manslaughter charge. Whatever it would be, it definitely wouldn't be capital murder. The jury, the Judge, and everyone following the case would know it was the drug's fault, not yours. Of course, there would be no way to exonerate all the repercussions, because it was your own free will to take them, but in everyone's eyes that mattered, you would be simply the by-product of the drug — you wouldn't have known what you were doing."

Meyers made two fists that turned his knuckles white. "Dontcha see that you'd be saving yourself many, many years in prison, and the electric chair wouldn't even come into the picture. There wouldn't be a jury in the country that would send you up the river very far, and given your squeaky clean past, and promising future, hell, you'd probably only spend two or three years in a minimum security prison and then be out on parole."

The suggestion felt like a hot knife ripping into John's chest. Despite the arrow looking like a dead end, he knew that the two men sitting across the table from him still thought that he was a murderer. John clearly understood Meyers' proposal — even if he hadn't been zonked out of his skull, this was a good chance for him not to spend the rest of his life in prison . . . or worse. Triplett might have to be talked into it, but Meyers was sneaky enough to make sure the report would read that John was impaired when it all went down.

Admittedly, the bargain did sound tempting. It was almost comical as John pictured himself sitting in some college class in a striped prison jumpsuit handcuffed to some overweight guard who suffered from an interminable case of BO. Maybe things were lenient enough in a minimum security prison to still allow him to go to school? But what the two investigators thought had happened out in those woods was a long ways from what actually happened. The truth that would acquit John altogether was hiding out in the woods somewhere in southern Jessup County. The armadillo blood was a small win, but Meyers and Triplett needed something else; perhaps just a glimpse of something that might give them a reason to believe. To dig deeper.

John bristled. "No! I've never done anything like that. Dad would have killed me. I don't believe it would be possible anyway. He kept all his samples locked in the trunk of the company car, and as I said before, he kept an unbelievably tight log on what and how much he had. And even if I could have managed to get some, I wouldn't, because when he found out the stuff was missing, I would have been the first person he would have landed on. You wouldn't have to threaten me with the electric chair, because he would have killed me right where I stood. And for the last time, I didn't kill my friends."

Detective Triplett looked surprised, and he leaned back in the chair, nearly falling off the seat. But the Captain never blinked. "Well, we might just have to take a look at it for ourselves then. A blood test is how we discovered it in the armadillo — we could use the same thing to find it in you."

John returned the Captain's cold stare. "Fine by me. You can waste your time if you like."

***

While John and Meyers were having their staring contest, Triplett centered himself back on his chair, and glanced at his watch. "My, my. Would you look at the time." He began gathering up the loose papers on the desk and when they were all in order, he stopped, straightened in his seat, and snapped his fingers. He saw both contestants cut their eyes at him, abandoning the game.

"I nearly forgot. John, could I please see your hands?"

"What?"

"Your hands. Let me take a look at them."

John raised them off his lap and sat them palm down on the table. "Like this?"

"No." Triplett stood and raised his arms in front of him, palms down, fingers spread. His thumbs nearly touched. "More like this."

John stood and complied, and Triplett leaned in, closely looking at the backs of his hands.

Triplett said in a low voice, nearly a mumble, "No discoloration or bruising, hmmm."

He held his hands up again, this time close to John's, but just before he touched them he smiled and asked, "Do you mind?"

Triplett watched as John glanced at Captain Meyers. The Marlboro was hanging loosely from his lip, like he was watching a very bad amateur magic trick. John's own face wrinkled as it turned back to Triplett's. It was if he, too, was watching the same trick. John shook his head slowly, the poster boy of confusion. Triplett lightly flipped them over, inspecting the palms. When he was finished, he gently squeezed them, making sure to compress both the kid's fingers and palms. John just stared at him blankly, and then Triplett did the same thing again, this time firmer, almost grinding the finger and hand bones together like a joke handshake.

Meyers said in a condescending tone, "What are you doing, detective?"

Triplett squeezed once more, then released John's hands. "I'm checking his hands for bruising and soreness."

Meyers' cigarette nearly fell from his mouth. "What for?"

"You saw the pictures. Those men were battered and bruised all over." He raised his hands curling them into a fist then straightening them to full extension. "If he was the one hitting them, he couldn't have stood what I just did."

Meyers looked at him. "I'll be damned."

***

The door to the Sheriff's office opened and both investigators walked out into the parking lot. The sun was dipping behind the courthouse, and the cool breeze rattled the bare limbs on the dogwoods planted around the square. Meyers bunched his collar close to his neck and followed the detective to his state issued Crown Victoria. Meyers leaned against the fender, tracing a crack in the corner of the windshield with his finger while Triplett dropped his briefcase in the backseat. Meyers wanted to ask him a lot of things, but decided to keep it simple.

"I know you're probably in a hurry to get back, but if you have a few minutes to spare, I'd like to ask you something."

Triplett straightened, waiting for it.

"The Sheriff asked you this morning what you thought of him." Meyers chinned back toward the office, "Well, what do you think about him now?"

Triplett ran fingers through his hair and shook his head. "He's a strange one, all right."

"What are you thinking?"

"I'm probably not telling you anything you don't already know, Captain, but in a perfect world, when someone tells a story like that, there's usually something

that stands out that makes it easy to unravel. You know —
inconsistency, a jumbled or transposed segment, maybe
an entire part of it that's new, or omitted, just because they
forget where they are in the lie, and what I see more than
anything else, a break or screw-up in the timeline. But this
young fellow is so solid, it's nearly scary."

Meyers nodded, looked down and kicked the tire. "I
don't see how he's doing it."

"I don't know either. It sure looks like he's the one
behind it, but somehow, he's either good enough to totally
commit to a fabrication like that, or he's completely
blocked out what actually happened. I've read accounts
about stuff like that in psychological journals. Sometimes
when a person commits an extraordinarily heinous act of
terror, the sane part of their mind, if there's any part left
that's sane, is able to block out the whole episode. From
what I understand, it something like a built-in sub-
conscious defense mechanism. I'm just speculating though
— that kind of stuff is better left to a shrink than me. But
what's really odd is that he looks genuinely sorry, even
frightened at times talking about it. It's like he's convinced
himself that's what happened. You remember him crying
when he got to the part when they all died? Those tears
and that reaction looked remarkably genuine."

"I was over in Atlanta for a while when I first started
this law enforcement business. Over there I saw rapes,
murders, robberies, assaults — pretty much any and every
rotten and despicable thing a human being can do to
another on a weekly basis. I think this takes the cake."

"I know what you mean. It was a few years before my
time, but when I first started at the Bureau, my supervisor
told me about a case he worked in the early eighties. I'm

reminded of it every time I see a teen with a messed up head."

"Oh yeah, what happened?"

"It was up in Decatur. A pretty little high school junior had a rough day at school just before Christmas break. Boyfriend break-up, failed an exam, grueling basketball practice — then she went home and found her mom sprawled out on the kitchen floor, beaten black and blue, bleeding from a gunshot wound in the belly. Broken home, single mother, latest attempt at finding Mr. Right, you know, the usual. Well, this girl was a rock, helping the EMT's out with everything, even rode to Huntsville to the trauma unit in the back of the ambulance holding her mom's hand the whole way. After a few hours in surgery, she was told that her mother would live, but they couldn't save her baby sister."

Triplett shook his head, "I remember the exact quote from the report. This young girl, I believe her name was Emily, glares at them for a moment, then calmly asks, 'What baby sister?' Well, she seems to get over it, and sits around for a while in a daze, and then walks over to the payphone in the lobby and secretly calls Mr. Right. She meets him at a gas station a couple of blocks away, and a witness said the guy walked out of the store with a twelve pack of beer in one hand, and the girl's ass in the other. So, the scumbag's knocked up the mother, and has taken care of it in his own wicked way, and now he's thinking that a double dip from the daughter is a sure thing. Well, he was wrong. Dead wrong. The next morning they pulled his car out of the Tennessee River under the I-65 Bridge. The front wheels were jacked way to the right, and when they pried open the door, this poor girl's hands were still tugging on the steering wheel from the passenger seat."

Meyers' jaw went slack. After a couple of attempts, he finally said, "So she gets revenge, but takes herself out in the process?"

Triplett smiled grimly and said, "Every time I think I've got somebody figured out, I go back and re-read that case. I always walk away with a renewed appreciation of how bitter, strange, and dangerous the human mind can be . . . not necessarily in that order."

Chapter 2

The Jessup County Sheriff's office was a homely brick building situated across the street from the main doors of the county courthouse, one of many equally dull buildings that guarded the town square. It hadn't always been that way though. Halifax survived the depression, and was vaulted into the post war boom doing what it did best, growing cotton. The big plantations that dotted the landscape for miles around the county seat could only believe that the world would always need cotton, and for many years that belief made the well-to-do families that were able to hold on during the hard times even richer. The need for cotton was insatiable, and the town and county flourished, but what they hadn't banked on was a pesky little insect called the boll weevil. Without warning and seemingly overnight, affected farms went from bumper crops to bumper busts. With little to no income, creditors started screaming, and one by one, the remnants of the old south started folding. Halifax once again braced for impact, but savvy farm managers started realizing there was yet another cash crop growing in and around those ruined fields. It was a little brown bird called the Bobwhite quail.

For most of the sixties, and all of the seventies, from October to March, Halifax was as busy as New Orleans during Mardi Gras. It wasn't unusual to see license plates from as far away as California parked neatly along the streets in front of the hotels. Scores of corporate big wigs, and Wall Street investment types descended on Jessup County carrying expensive double-guns and wanting to ride horses or horse-drawn wagons through the piney woods following sleek bird dogs. While it lasted, things were good — almost as good as it had been during the cotton boom, but when those little brown birds began to wane, the big money did likewise. What remained was just a shadow of its former self, but the quail and cotton didn't die-out completely, and neither did Halifax.

The town survived, but the luxury of big municipal budgets became just a dream, and the city council, more interested in utility than aesthetics, made the austere architecture mandatory. The Sheriff's office, along with all the other vessels of city and county government, and private commerce were hopelessly bound to exist with similar, if not identical, structure and color. An outsider driving through Halifax probably would think the county seat was just one big eye-sore, but to county regulars: merchants, law enforcement and justice officials, and citizens that regularly conducted business there, it had simply become what was downtown Halifax.

The inside of the Sheriff's Office, in a lot of ways, was equally unimpressive. The lobby, furnished with an unfortunate combination of burnt orange shag carpet and beige wallpaper, smelled of stale cigarette smoke intermingled with a hint of mothballs. Staring at each other from opposite walls were archaic portraits of Generals Robert E. Lee, and George Washington, both mounted on horseback, sabers in hand. The only conveniences were two chairs and a dirty couch that surrounded a small coffee table in the center of the room. The table held a plain white ashtray, and what most people in the county considered fine cultured reading: two copies each of months old *Field and Stream,* and *Southern Living.*

On the far wall, a sliding window, a design stolen from every doctor's office, stood partway open, and every day from six to six Judy Thornton sat behind it, ready for whatever madness the reprobates of the county could produce. Miss Judy, as everyone called her, was a plump, older lady with thinning blue hair. She had retired from the bank across the street a decade ago, but chose to spend her golden years making minimum wage directing visitors, answering the phone, and running dispatch for the office.

To the left of the window, in the corner, stood a small Christmas tree that Miss Judy erected each December, and to the right stood a door which opened to a long hallway, leading into the bowels of Jessup County's law enforcement machine. It was down this hallway, a few minutes past 6:00 a.m., where Deputy Andy Williams walked, carrying a small covered aluminum tray and a glass of orange juice. He passed the door to Sheriff Butters' office then stopped in total surprise at the Captain's door. Meyers, who usually came in at 7:00, was already armpit deep in the Bateman file.

"Good morning, sir. I see you're getting an early start this morning."

Meyers looked up from his notes, tapping his chin with the pencil eraser. "I suppose that's what you'd call it." He straightened and stretched his back, and catching a glance at the wall calendar, he said out loud, "Tuesday, January 5th." The Captain turned back to the deputy as if to explain the sudden interest in the date. "I was hoping to get in early and spend a couple of peaceful hours re-digesting this Bateman stuff before the mayhem started, but it's just not happening. It feels all wrong — like how the air feels when a storm is coming." He rolled his head around on his neck, trying to relax stiff muscles. "You ever get bad feelings like that?"

Deputy Williams shrugged his shoulders. "I guess. Every now and again."

"Well, I've had that feeling crawling all over me since I walked through the door." Meyers shook a finger at the calendar. "I don't know how I know it, but I think it's going to be one helluva Tuesday."

"Well, good luck with it, sir. If I can help with anything, let me know."

Meyers noticed the tray, "That for the boy?"

The deputy nodded. "Straight from the Butters' residence. I picked it up on the way in."

The Captain turned back to the mountain of papers on his desk. "Well go ahead and deliver. He was asleep when I came in, and probably still is, but it's time for our young hunter to come to life back there. And unless you have something pressing, stay with him for a little while. I need some more time with all this without anyone in my hair."

★

Deputy Williams rapped loudly on the iron bars, as he turned the key, opening the cell door. He sat the plate down on the edge of the cot and thumped John on the shoulder. "Rise and shine. Mrs. Sheriff Butters sends her regards along with breakfast this morning."

The deputy peeled back the tinfoil, and John surveyed the offering through narrow slits in his eyelids. There were two eggs, fried and still runny in the middle, four pieces of narrow bacon that were more fat than lean, and a couple of pieces of toast that on second glance looked more like replacement roof shingles than sustenance. Beside the tray sat the small glass of orange juice, or what was supposed to be orange juice. It was too pale to be the real thing. It wasn't much of a breakfast, but for the first time since Sunday, John felt like eating. Rubbing his eyes, he thanked the deputy, and noticed his name on left breast pocket.

"Has there been any word from my folks, Deputy Williams?"

Williams looked like he was keeping a secret. John recognized it and pressed. "Don't worry, I won't tell anyone if you tell me something that you aren't supposed to. Even if I did, they'd probably not believe me anyway."

Williams thought for a moment, then smiled. "Well, since you put it that way, yeah, your dad called late yesterday evening. Somewhere in St. Louis I believe they said."

"Yeah, he's had to take care of some business up there, and mom went with him — said they'd probably be back by Thursday if everything went well, Friday if things got messy. Do you know what he said?"

"He talked to Captain Meyers. I didn't get all of it because I was only catching half of the conversation, but from what I could hear it sounded like he was satisfied that you had not been accused yet, and understands what role you are supposed to be playing regarding the case. He knows you are supposed to be cooperating with us on every level."

John noticed a hint of sarcasm and could see disbelief in the deputy's eyes.

Deputy Williams balled the tinfoil up in his hands, "Everyone here knows your dad, so I think it's understood that we wouldn't change your status of P.O.I. to suspect without him knowing it." The young deputy stared blankly at the wall and shrugged his shoulders, "If that happens, I'm not sure exactly what would be the next step. I imagine we'd just start from scratch, except this time, lawyers would be involved." His eyes went back to John, still staring at the tray of food. "The Sheriff talked with your folks when all this started. They understand what is happening here. I do know they are anxious to come home to be with you and to help figure it all out, it's just the weather up there has everything locked-up."

John picked up the piece of toast, looked at it, and dropped it back onto the tray. It clinked loudly against the aluminum. A little surprised, he envisioned his father on the brink of declaring war with all involved parties. Maybe Clay was more upset than he let on to Butters, but then again, he was always cool under pressure. John picked up the glass and sipped the pale juice. He made a face before continuing, "What's going on with the weather up there? I remember something on the news just before they left about the chance for a few snow showers, but I haven't been able to see the news since we left to go hunting."

Deputy Williams said, "The chance for snow shot through the roof Friday night. The cold front barreling in from the north didn't stall over Iowa like they were predicting. It just kept on trucking down through all of Missouri. They were hammered in St. Louis with something just shy of a full-fledged blizzard."

John's appetite sank like a stone in a well, and around a piece of half chewed bacon he asked, "What'd he say about Al and the others?"

"Nothing much, I think he was still in shock."

John picked up the plastic fork, cut into a runny egg, and watched the warm yellow gel ooze from the center. It reminded him of what Renn's head looked like when they found him. He blinked back the image and tried to eat, but gagged a little, wondering if eggs and brains shared any commonality. When it finally went down, he asked, "Did he want to talk to me?"

"Yes, he did. In fact, the Captain was on his way back here to get you, but I stopped him. I had just come through, and I saw that you were actually getting a little shut-eye. He got back on the phone and asked Clay if he should wake you up, and from what I could hear, the answer to that was no, just to let you sleep for now, and he'd call back and talk to you first thing in the morning."

John tried another piece of bacon. "That's this morning, right?"

The deputy nodded

"I wonder what he'll say?" But as he chewed John didn't say what he was really thinking. After telling and re-telling the story, it was obvious that Triplett and Meyers would just as soon believe that a homicidal Sasquatch with an archery fetish was running loose in the woods down there than some crazed buck deer. The looks both men had given him were easy to decipher. What John needed more than anything now were allies. Meyers seemed to be a lost cause, and it was doubtful that he'd ever win Triplett over. So the real question now was whether Clayton and Layla Bateman would believe him.

Chapter 3

After John finished breakfast, Captain Meyers escorted him into another small room. It wasn't the same interrogation room he was in the day before; this new room was home to a few more comforts, three of which John appreciated very much. His chair was padded, instead of just cold, hard wood, the room itself was larger than a cozy coffin, and there was no two-way mirror. As a bonus, John noticed that the clock beside the door was operating normally, and it read what he assumed was the correct time.

To John's surprise, Captain Meyers was smiling. There seemed to be an air of compassion floating around him that was nowhere to be found those first two days. He even offered John a glass of milk before he sat down and opened another folder.

"Good morning John. It looks like you might have been able to get a little sleep last night."

John nodded, taking a sip.

Meyers laid a small stack of papers on the desk, then said, "Yesterday evening we brought up a little matter of a blood test. Well, we can't take one from you legally without your permission or permission from your folks." The Captain's eyes moved to the stack of papers between them, and he tapped the top one with a pen he produced from his shirt pocket. "I have the form and a pen right here. If you feel the same way this morning as yesterday, you can sign it now and we can go ahead and get this out of the way. I want to warn you though, if there is any reason at all why you wouldn't want —"

Before Meyers finished the sentence, John grabbed the pen, gave the form a good once-over, and signed and dated it.

"I figured that's what you were going to do. Good. We can go ahead and get this done first thing. The quick and easy way to find out for sure if you have any traces of that zol . . . zolpi . . . baahhh. Whatever that substance was we found in the armadillo's blood."

John politely corrected Meyers. "Zolpidem, or better yet, Bipferin."

"Okay, whatever its name was. Anyway, you'll have to forgive me for being a little presumptuous. After our conversation about it wrapping up yesterday, I assumed that you'd agree to it again this morning. The nurse is here from Montgomery — she pulled in a few minutes ago. And before you start again about how this is all just a monumental waste of time, you need to remember that this is all just S.O.P. Whenever we find drugs in someone or in this case *something* that it's not supposed to be in, we have to perform drug tests. Being that this is a triple homicide investigation, we'd probably have ordered one whether we knew drugs were part of it or not."

The door opened, and Deputy Williams escorted not one, but two ladies into the room. Immediately John's blood pressure spiked. It was Joni Thompson, Marissa's mom, and following closely behind was Marissa. John could feel his heart beating in his neck. Both were dressed in scrubs with 'East Montgomery Medical Center' insignia embroidered in pink lettering above the left breast pocket. Of all the nurses in all the hospitals they could have called, they had to pick her, he thought. Or had been the other way around? Either way, a bad feeling began to grow in the pit of his stomach. If word hadn't gotten out about it yet, it surely would now, just as soon as they made it back to Montgomery.

Meyers gave them a quick once over, then as if satisfied that they had met some personal appearance approval, and didn't appear to be harboring weapons or desire to otherwise spring his person of interest, he seemed to relax and said, "Would you ladies please stand over here against the table, feet shoulder width apart."

Joni motioned to Marissa to stand still, and cut a poisoned eye at the Captain. "We were frisked and cleared in the lobby a little while ago. I'm a happily married woman, and I don't like the idea of being groped to death in here just trying to get a blood sample. It was Deputy Williams who had the honor of checking my crotch for files and guns. I'm sure he'll vouch for both of us."

Meyers made a sour face, and after he cleared his throat to sound more macho he asked, "Why does it take two nurses to take a blood sample?"

Joni smiled as she opened her tray, revealing sample tubes, syringes, and hypodermic needles, all packed neatly in sterile clear plastic bags. When she was finished, she looked at Marissa and said, "Well Tiffany, I don't know about you, but I don't think I've ever been greeted so warmly in all my life. Tell me dear, are we still in the south?"

"My apologies Ma'am. My name is Jonas Meyers, lead investigator for Jessup County. May I bid you good morning?"

"Now, that's sounds more like how a gentlemen is supposed to address a couple of ladies, deputy."

Color burst across the investigator's cheeks. "That's Captain, Ma'am. Captain Jonas Meyers."

Joni hid a wink to Marissa and said, "Oh, I'm terribly sorry Captain. I didn't mean to demote you like that. But to answer your question, my name is Joni Thompson, and this is Tiffany Odom. She's a freshman in the nursing program at UAB, and is doing an internship with us this semester. She needs twenty-five sticks for class credit, and it was mighty slow at the hospital this morning, so when we got the word that you needed a sample taken, we volunteered. Kinda killing two birds with one stone, you see. I needed the fresh air and change of scenery, and Tiffany here needed to go vein diving. We couldn't lose."

Captain Meyers looked at the ceiling and scratched his chin. "Seems like I knew a Joni back in high school. She was a pretty little thing. Wavy brown hair, green eyes, basketball player, I believe. Joni — I always did like that name."

Joni, who was looking at Marissa (Tiffany Odom by nametag) rolled her eyes at the overly apparent flirt, and opened a package and withdrew a large syringe. It was at least six inches long, and Meyers' eyes immediately widened. Then she opened another package and removed a large needle. It was almost as long as the syringe. Meyers blinked wildly while Joni affixed the needle on the syringe. The Captain's legs quivered and he said, "Well, uhm, well, if, uhm . . . if it's all the same to you Ma'am, I think I'll go outside for a smoke while you two are drilling for oil."

John looked concerned and was starting to pale, but when the door shut with Meyers safely on the other side,

Joni laid the large syringe down and quickly assembled a smaller one. John breathed a sigh of relief. Instead of looking like she was about to stab him in the chest to take the sample straight from his left ventricle, the new needle seemed much more appropriate for the task of drawing a simple blood sample.

While she prepped his arm, Marissa walked to the door and put her ear against it. Satisfied, she walked back over and whispered, "What in the world is going on, John? We heard yesterday that you had been arrested for murder. Something about your dad's hunting friends. What did you do? What happened?"

John quickly told the story again, and included the part about the trace drugs found in the armadillo blood. When he was finished, he corrected Marissa. He had not technically been arrested, but it was looking like that might happen sooner than later.

Both Marissa and her mother just stood there, mouths open, visibly shocked.

John noticed the look and said, "I don't blame you for not believing me. Heck, I can hardly believe it myself."

"A deer did all that?" Marissa looked like she had just been told the punchline to every joke that she would hear for the rest of her life.

"I saw it with my own two eyes, and if it hadn't been for a rickety deer stand, I wouldn't be here now either. That big son of a gun almost had me, but the way things are looking around here, I might've been better off if he had."

Joni surveyed the bend in John's arm closely, hesitated, then slowly pushed the needle through the skin and into a vein. While the sample syringe filled, she said, "Don't say that John. I can believe it. I've seen some off the wall stuff like this at the hospital. They've brought dog attack victims in with arms and legs nearly torn off. And while they are being sewn back together, they mumble stuff about how ole Buster never hurt a flea in his life.

"And don't tell me that sudden attacks haven't happened with wild animals before. What about the so-called trained bears and elephants you read about in the circuses? They are happy as clams doing their act, then somebody in the crowd hollers something or wears the wrong color combination and it sets them off, and half the folks in the first five rows get maimed."

She looked down at the sample tube that was now nearly full. She lightly tapped it, waited a few moments, then removed that one and affixed another.

John didn't understand. "Why are you taking two samples?"

"Well, we had to run Captain Weak Knees out of the room didn't we? I still need to make it look good. I'm gonna draw a second vial and put it in that big honkin' syringe. Gonna leave it right on the tray when I walk out too. That ought to sell it good."

John smiled, "How did you know he didn't like blood or needles?"

"I was the Joni he remembered from high school. I didn't think he would recognize me. He was several grades ahead, and I wouldn't have been a blip on his radar screen then . . . not that I wanted to be. He was sorta goofy, even back then. From the looks of things, not much has changed. He was a tough character though — I remember him getting blistered one day playing soft ball. Somebody cracked a line-drive, and drilled him right in the snoz. He took it like a prizefighter, only staggering a little, but went down like a sack of potatoes when he wiped the back of his hand across his upper lip and saw blood. He was squeamish about it back then, and well, I just took a chance that he hadn't changed. Did you see how he looked when I took that long needle out? He almost fainted."

"So did I."

The second sample filled, and Joni backed the needle out, and transferred the contents into the joke syringe. "Look, we are going to fix you up. I don't care if you were on something or not, we are going to make this blood sample look as clean as the Pope's."

John shook his head while holding a clean piece of gauze on the needle mark. "Don't worry. You aren't going to find anything in that blood sample but blood. I'm no druggie, but I might need to be. According to Weak Knees, it might be a good thing if something *was* in it."

"What?" Marissa and Joni both said it at the same time.

"He said I'd have a better chance with a jury if I was high on something when all of this went down."

Marissa gasped. "Are you serious? The Captain told you that?"

"I couldn't believe it either at first. He said that I'd likely not go to prison for very long if I was on something. I could claim that I didn't know what I was doing. It would explain this whole mess a lot better. I saw what I saw out there, but I don't know what it's gonna take for them to believe it." John tenderly wiped a tear off Marissa's cheek. "The way he was talking, it wouldn't surprise me if the Captain asks the folks at whatever lab this ends up at to make sure the results show that a chemical called zolpidem is in my blood. He thinks he'll be doing me a favor. I doubt he'll say anything to you, but if you deliver it to wherever it's going, please to tell them what's up, and that they might expect a note or a call from the Captain sometime. No matter how it shakes out, I want to keep this on the level. I can't let my dad think I'm a junkie."

Joni said, "Speaking of Clayton, have you and your dad had a chance to talk?" I heard on the news that Missouri was hit hard with snow. Are they on their way back?"

"I don't think so. One of the deputies told me the airport is frozen solid, and no, we haven't spoken yet. He's supposed to call sometime this morning. He doesn't know it, but I think he's going to help me more than he knows. It's kinda weird. Dad had to go fix a botched shipment, and it seems that a drug his company handles has all of a sudden appeared down here in Jessup County."

Marissa said, "You mean what they found in the armadillo was something that your dad's company deals with?"

"Crazy ain't it? I don't know if it's going to be the same drug that went missing or not? I suppose I'll find out when I talk with him. Whether it is or it isn't, they're all thinking that I'm the one who got it down there . . . the vector. I'll swear on a stack of Bibles that I've never fooled with any of that stuff. But it's pretty obvious that somebody down here has."

Joni arranged all the medical equipment back into her tray, everything except the large joke syringe, now nearly glowing bright red. She left it on top in clear view. Marissa hugged John and buried her face in his chest. "Oh, John, I still can't believe you're mixed up in this mess." She backed away, then advanced again and did something that John wasn't expecting. On her tip-toes, she leaned forward, and planted a wet kiss on his lips. John felt an active tongue waggle across his teeth. Encouraged, he slipped his own past puckered lips, and both made small intertwining circles, tasting each other's youth.

Joni tapped Marissa's shoulder. "All right missy, no need to put the boy in orbit just yet. Besides, we've got work to do."

Marissa withdrew, and she and her mother made their way to the door while John was attempting to hide his eagerness. Marissa went out first, but Joni turned back and caught John mid-adjustment. "Don't worry about Weak Knees. We are headed over there right now to deliver your sample to the forensics lab, and I'll make sure to tell them what you said." Joni glanced down and smiled. "Oh and John, you might want to watch where you point that thing."

John's face was crimson. "Thanks Mrs. Thompson," was all he could say.

Captain Meyers was pale when he came back in. "I wish she would have covered that 55 gallon drum of a syringe with something. I could have gone all day not seeing that."

When his color returned, he said, "John, you have a phone call. It's your Father."

Chapter 4

John's prediction about the conversation with his father couldn't have been more true. The Captain walked him through the door, sat him down at a corner of his desk, handed him the handset, and immediately Clay's angry, miniature telephone voice exploded across the room. Meyers looked amused, while John winced, listening to the tirade. Several minutes passed, and the only things that came from the kid were numerous yes-sirs and no-sirs. After a while, Clay's rage calmed and John was finally able to talk.

As much as he wanted to, John couldn't hide his end of the conversation, and after the obvious had been covered, the discussion shifted more to Clayton's work and his frustration at being three states away. Meyers was trying to piece it together from what John was saying and the snippets he could understand filtering through the phone line, and he quickly shifted his notebook into a better writing position, while leaning forward and cocking an ear towards the phone.

John felt almost secondary to the fact that on one hand, his father was going on and on about some sizeable order mix-up that Kirby had been the lead on, and on the other, the Captain was constantly scribbling useless notes about several cases of missing drugs. He almost handed the phone to Meyers, just to cut out the middle-man, but something tripped his mental switch. He heard his father say that out of the three missing cases, they had only managed to track down a single case of prescription cough medicine that somehow wound up in east Texas. And the other cases of sedatives had just vanished, and that all the inventories and back-tracking had been just one massive dead end with absolutely nothing to go on . . . not even a cold paper trail.

Watching Meyers write, John said into the phone, "I know it's hard to be mad at him now, dad. You don't have to apologize for having to go out there and straighten out that mess."

The handset continued to buzz with Clay's irritated voice.

"Yes, sir. I hope you find out what happened to the rest of it too. It's hard to believe that cases of drugs can just turn up missing like that. Maybe the rest of them are somewhere between St. Louis and Texas and you just haven't located them yet? You did say this was Kirby's order, right?"

Meyers, still listening, scribbled in the notebook.

"Sure, sure, I understand that things can easily go wrong with the forms, and I'm sure that you can track it all down."

. . .

No, don't worry about me Dad. I'll be okay here for now."

. . .

"Yes, they're treating me okay."

. . .

"No, the only thing they have made me do is tell em' the story several times. Oh, and they asked and I agreed to a drug test."

. . .

"No dad, it's fine. They aren't going to find anything. You know I don't mess with your samples."

. . .

"Yes sir, we'll figure it out."

. . .

"Tell Mom I love her too."

John hung up the phone. There was one more question he wanted to ask his father, but he purposefully omitted it. There was just too much of an audience there at Meyers' desk. He thought for a moment, then turned to the Captain and looked as if he had hit his thumb with a hammer.

Meyers saw it and asked, "What's wrong, John?"

"I forgot to ask him something. Can I call him back, if not now maybe in a little bit?"

"You can try, but I believe he was calling from a pay phone from the airport. Do you know where he was staying, and what room he's in?"

John had the number to the Gateway Inn folded up in his wallet in the rear pocket of his orange jumpsuit, but if he tried to call now, Meyers would still be there listening. No, he needed to wait until he could talk in private, or at least without somebody sitting within arm's reach.

"Mom left me all that contact info for me. It's on the fridge at home, and we had it down at hunting camp. I really need to call him back."

Meyers propped his elbows on the desk, and mindlessly twisted the wedding band on his finger. "I've got a couple of the deputies down there right now meeting the towing guys. I'll raise them on the radio and get them to look for it. I'd bet next month's pay that Clay is at this very moment cussing the lady at the ticket window for not having any de-iced flights back to Birmingham. We'll give him a little while, and when the deputies get back, we'll try him back at the hotel."

***

Besides not answering the questions the way they wanted him to, John followed all the protocol inside the Sheriff's office to the letter. As a sign of good faith, Butters issued new orders, allowing him roaming privileges inside the office . . . provided there was a deputy close by at all times. It was better than any Christmas present John ever received. Being confined in that cramped holding cell was sheer torture, so, trying to be as amiable as possible, John spent most of his free time quietly observing Jessup County's big wheel of justice rolling merrily along its daily routine from the quaintness of Captain Meyers' small office. Down the hall, he could hear Miss Judy banging away on a typewriter, and taking calls. Through the window that overlooked the big open space that was home to the deputy's workstations, he watched one of the night shift deputies cleaning his side-arm at his desk. Another deputy was completing impounding forms for Al's and Kirby's vehicles that were presumably on the way back to Halifax, and Sheriff Butters occasionally would walk by, filling and refilling his coffee mug at the makeshift kitchenette further down the hall. Even with a triple homicide case pending, it was apparent that law enforcement in Jessup County this time of the year was as dull as the shag carpeting in the lobby.

Thirty mind-numbing minutes later, Captain Meyers downed the last of his fifth cup of coffee, then made his way down the hall to the restroom. John saw the chance and motioned at the deputy who was finished with the pistol, and now seemed to be just shuffling papers back and forth across the desk.

Deputy Stanley Brooks poked his head in the door, yawned and said, "You need something?"

"Yeah, I just thought about my dog. I wanted to see if I could call one of my friends to see if he'd swing by and check on him. He stays in a pen behind the house, and has one of those gravity fed automatic feeders. He's turned that thing over before, and it doesn't work unless it's standing up. It's kinda like a gumball machine. Have you ever tried to get a piece of gum out of one of those things lying on its side? I just want to make sure Sambo isn't going hungry.

The deputy scratched his head and said, "I suppose that'll be fine." He pointed at the phone on Meyers' desk. "Go ahead and use the Captain's there if you like."

John thought for a moment. "Well, I was hoping to stretch my legs a little too. Do you mind if I take a couple of laps up and down the hall, and then — hey there's a phone on the wall by the coffee maker, isn't there?"

"Sure is. Make it quick though, I was about to head home to give the day-shift boys a chance to fight crime today. I'll be at my desk if you need me. Just dial the number straight. There's no code or anything."

John quickly made a lap, then headed straight for the phone. He pulled the slip of paper from his wallet, dialed, and Clay answered on the first ring.

"Hey Dad — I forgot something while ago."

"Well, what is it? And does it involve a way to de-ice a small Delta jet and a half-mile of runway so we can get home?"

"It doesn't, sorry about that. I wanted to ask you what kind of drugs were in the mix-up?"

"Bipferin, mostly."

John had to hold onto the wall to keep from falling. Somehow, the same drug that was missing from their St. Louis warehouse had found its way into an armadillo in south Alabama. The possibilities swam through his head, and what was first just a reasonable coincidence now seemed like a solid possibility. His mind could only think of one name. Kirby. Kirby was working the shipment for the company, and he was down there hunting — he had proximity to all of it. Was he the missing puzzle piece . . . the connection?

John blinked a few times running the scenario around in the attic. "Dad, I think I know were the shipment went."

"Now how the devil would you know that?"

The phone went silent for a long moment. John could almost hear the gears grinding in his father's mind, considering all the information. It finally started sinking in.

"No way! I don't believe it. You're kidding me, right? Kirby? Kirby wouldn't do anything like that. He'd lose his job for one thing. And we are talking about enough of this stuff to knock out a whole wing of death-row inmates waiting for the needle. Two cases is a lot of Bipferin. How much of it did they find in the armadillo?"

"Only a trace."

Clay huffed, "Not much more than a trace should have shut something that small down indefinitely. How would you even get an armadillo to ingest it anyway?"

"I have no idea, but I don't think Kirby would go through that much trouble and risk just to have some fun getting an armadillo high."

The line fell silent again, then the two possibilities were there in the teen's mind as clear as the water that flowed through Indian Mound Creek. "Two cases, huh? Dad, I wonder if Kirby was trying to sell some of that stuff down here, or maybe even get some of that stuff into that big buck he had on the game cameras. The one he believed would be the next state record."

Clay was three steps behind John's pace, but was catching up fast. "Well, he wasn't married, and had no kids, but he did have a pretty little niece via a sister and brother-in-law. He talked about her all the time — loved her like she was his own. I doubt he'd stoop to sell that stuff to kids, but that buck might be a different story. He sure was tore up about him, wasn't he? But how would you go about getting it into a specific animal in eight hundred acres of timberlands? It's not like he could just leave the pills out there on a plate and expect him to walk right up to it and eat them."

"He must have mixed it with something. Corn, soybeans or maybe that sweet-feed that everyone feeds their goats and horses. He could have done that and baited up a few spots. Deer can find a corn pile in the woods lickety-split. Sooner or later that big buck would find it and get a good dose. Kirby had him on the game cameras, so he already knew where he was hanging out. Didn't you say it's used as some kind of relaxer?"

"Yeah, it's a sedative. Insomniacs take it to help them sleep. Some take it in smaller doses as a muscle relaxer."

"Do you think it would have the same effect on deer? Would it make it easier to kill them?"

"I suppose. If they'd get a good dose of that stuff, they wouldn't give a shit if you'd walk right up to them and slit their throat. I really don't think — I mean, I just can't see Kirby doing it." There was another pause then his father asked, "You really think he wanted to kill a deer so bad, he'd resort to this?"

"It's possible, I guess. Think about it for a minute. Even if that big buck didn't get enough of that stuff in him to knock him out, he might be chilled out enough to walk around the woods for a while with his guard down. Drunk people are easy enough to screw with, a drunk deer stumbling around in the woods should be easier to see . . . easier to kill. Hey, that might explain why that doe I shot and the doe that attacked that smaller buck were stumbling around too."

John stopped mid-thought. "Oh — my — God!"

"What's the matter?"

"We all ate the back loins for lunch! That doe from Saturday morning — if she had it in her, then we might all have gotten a dose from the meat! I didn't think of that, and I just gave a blood —"

Clay quickly put out the fire. "No, no. Don't worry about that. It doesn't work that way. Unless you ate it raw, there's no way it could have manifested in your system. High heat denatures the compound. There's no way that zolpidem could stay together when subjected to cooking temperatures for any amount of time."

"Are you sure?"

"Positive."

It was a load off John's mind, and when he could breathe again, he picked up where his train of thought so abruptly derailed. "You know, there's something about it that doesn't add up. If that drug was supposed to make them mellow out, why were they acting so wired up and crazy? Almost like it had the opposite effect?

"Well the pharmaceutical industry doesn't perform drug trials on Whitetail deer, so we wouldn't know exactly how they would take it. Deer and humans have basically the same metabolic functions though, so I don't think it would be too far of a stretch to assume that they would have similar responses to it."

They both silently considered the possibilities. After a moment, John said, "Well, these deer are rutting, and battling each other over the females; they are literally reeking of testosterone. You think that might make a difference?"

"I dunno. It might, but that wouldn't explain why the doe was aggressive, unless it acts on estrogen similarly."

The thought lingered, and John could hear someone in the background through the phone line. He thought at first it might be his mom, but it was the lady meteorologist on television in motel room giving the latest snowfall amounts.

His mom!

For the first time since it all started, John thought of Layla Bateman. She was an incredibly strong woman, but there was no way she could be taking all this too well. "How's mom doing?"

"Not too good. In fact, she took a little something a little while ago to help her rest some. She hasn't slept since we first got the call."

"Tell her I'm sorry —"

Before he could finish, Clay said, "Don't worry about her right now. She'll be fine. The best thing you can do for her is to figure a way out of all this. Talk to Jonas and that Triplett guy. Tell them to look for bags or buckets — something that Kirby could have used to mix and carry the bait in. Tell Jonas I said that if he wants a bid for Sheriff one day, he'll at least give us the benefit of the doubt. If Kirby did steal those cases and laced the corn or whatever it was and tried to feed it to that buck, there will be traces of it somewhere. We have to have evidence that he was tampering with that stuff. I wish I could be there to help in person, but this weather has us so bottled up here we can't go or come. You do what you can down there and I'll check on the clinical trials they run on Bipferin. Maybe it has some screwy side effects? Between that and tracking those missing cases, at least I won't lose my mind from boredom here in this confounded motel room."

"Thanks, Dad. You were reading my mind. And I know exactly what you mean about not going anywhere."

John hung up the phone, and turned to see the Deputy Brooks walking back towards him from his desk.

"Is he going to do it?"

John looked lost. "Do what?"

"Check on your dog."

"Oh sure. He's going to do that right after lunch. Sorry about that, he was telling me about a date he had last night." John held both hands up to his chest, palms up, and shook invisible breasts.

The deputy smiled and looked eager. "Oh yeah! Well then, you might just have to tell me more about that later on. Might have something to do with these murders, and a good deputy must always exhaust every lead."

Brooks walked John straight to the holding cell and passed Captain Meyers on the way out carrying a briefcase. The Captain said, "I've got to step out for a little bit to deliver a file over at the DA's office. I'm probably going to catch an early lunch too, that is, if I can stay away from the newspaper reporter. Be back in a little while."

"Okay, sir. We'll keep everything covered on our end. I'm gonna deposit the kid back in his cell, and then help the others with the vehicles. I think they just rolled in."

When they made it to the cell, John saw that an early lunch had been delivered. It was a small grilled pork chop sandwich with French fries, and a couple of spoonfuls of baked beans. The bun had several small spots torn from it. It looked like a rat had a go at it before they brought it to him, or even more likely, Mrs. Butters had pinched off several spots of mold before sending it over. The beans were cold, the fries were stale, and the pork beneath the mangled bun was charred. It didn't matter to John though. He was excited about what had transpired with his dad, and with the excitement came hunger.

He chiseled off a hunk of sandwich, and attempted to chew. *Kirby didn't hunt with us that Friday evening, and he had to get that game camera film sometime earlier in the week. He was down there before we all showed up Friday afternoon. He could have done an awful lot of baiting then. He had to have the laced feed in something. Whatever he used, he must have had it in the suburban on the way down from Montgomery. So maybe that's why the back end of his Chevy was full! No wonder it looked like he was packing enough stuff to stay a month. If the deputies can find any kernels of corn or bags or buckets in the Suburban, they can test it for Bipferin. That has to be how that armadillo there at the camp house got into it. Kirby must have spilled some of the bait, or maybe he tossed the leftover bags in the bushes somewhere close by and the armadillo went nosing through it? Wait a minute — do armadillos eat corn? Now that's a stupid question, Johnny-boy. Armadillos will eat anything that doesn't eat them back.*

He tried to swallow, but it wouldn't go down. It was like trying to swallow a mouthful of gravel. He added a splash of Coke, and tried again, this time successfully. The picture still wasn't clear, but at least a few parts of it were starting to take shape. John looked at the clock. Triplett was supposed to be back from Montgomery at one o'clock. He would have to wait until then. Talking to the Captain about it would be worthless. He choked down the bite, and nearly laughed out loud. *If the Captain was half as tough as this pork chop, I would have confessed a long time ago.*

Chapter 5

Captain Meyers didn't know how right he was that morning when he waggled a finger at the calendar and said it was going to be one helluva Tuesday.

Meyers strolled through the doors of the Sheriff's office promptly at 5:00 a.m., a full two hours earlier than normal. He jokingly tipped his hat and said good morning to Robert and George hanging on the wall, then made his way down the hallway past the offices to the kitchenette. He filled his mug and looked in on John, sound asleep on the cot, then ambled back to his office, took a deep breath, and opened the Bateman file. He hoped that coming in early with a set of fresh eyes would have produced the break he needed; discovering something hidden in between the lines, interwoven amid the details they might have missed. He poured every ounce of himself into it for two and a half hours, but gained only the beginnings of a monumental headache. Quite simply, the Captain was hopelessly lost at a dead end.

The morning diversions, visits from the nurses and the Clay Bateman phone call, couldn't have come at a better time, giving his mind something else to do besides spin its bald tires all over hopeless paperwork. But even then, he knew that wasn't going to be enough. After John hung up the phone with his father, Meyers looked at his watch — 9:45. He had to find something else to do to pass the time and carry him through lunch, and after blankly staring at his messy desk, he knew what that something else was.

After cleaning and organizing his workspace, filing all the loose paperwork from the week before, reviewing the few upcoming cases that were scheduled for trial next week, and even walking down to the supply closet for a new notebook and pencils he looked at his watch again — 10:02. He frowned and thumped the crystal a few times, making sure it was still running. There was nothing else to do except wait on Triplett.

He wasn't going to sit in his office for three hours waiting for reinforcements, so he stuffed a briefcase under his arm for looks, and after bumping into John and Deputy Brooks in the hallway, he walked out the door to greet what was left of the morning. The fresh, crisp air slapped him in the face, and the brilliant blue sky stretched to all points of the compass above Halifax, without so much as an airliner's vapor trail to ruin its splendor. Until then, it hadn't been a good morning, but he managed a smile, as the smell of fresh pit cooked barbecue wafted on the breeze.

After a long lunch at Giggy Piggy's, and pleasant walk through town, Meyers turned back towards the Sheriff's Office. The wall clock in the lobby said 12:55, as he came through the main doors and made his way back down the long hallway to his office. He opened the door, and from across the small room, he could see the Bateman file laying by the phone, silently mocking him. The longer he stood there the more his mind receded into that dark place where things are not quite what they seem. He began to hear what sounded like whispers floating across the room from that wretched manila folder. Words like DUMMY, IDIOT, STUPID, IGNORAMOUS came to him again and again. For an embarrassing brief moment, Meyers actually let himself believe that the file was talking to him.

Maybe David is right? Maybe this case is starting to get to me?

Quickly he snapped out of it, shaking his head trying to clear the remaining cobwebs. Detective Triplett was supposed to be on his way, and there was nothing left to do except diving back into the kid's statement, hoping and praying that something new might magically jump from the pages. Nearly four hours had passed since he had closed the file earlier that morning . . . maybe that would be enough?

He was reaching for the file, when the desk phone rang. The Captain blew a sigh of relief as he answered it. "Jessup County Sheriff's office. Captain Jonas Meyers here."

A deep voice resonated on the other end of the line. "Captain Meyers, my name is Doctor Ronald Morris calling from the forensics lab at Auburn."

Meyers smiled, "Yes sir. I have been expecting either a call or fax from you."

"I apologize for the intrusion to your busy day, Captain. Someone from our staff of technicians usually follows up with the authorities when or if a phone call is warranted, but after getting this from you, it just didn't seem prudent for one of the wannabes to relay what I'm about to tell you. I have the results of your test, but there is something else I'd like to speak with you about. Something just from me to you — off the record."

"Well, what's on your mind, Mister Morris?"

"Doctor Morris —"

"Okay. What's on your mind, Doctor Morris?"

"Captain Meyers, It's not every day we get something from down your way. In fact, I had one of the interns look back at the records. She came up with exactly three items that have come from your office in the last five years. And now we get two orders in two days? Y'all are still in Jessup County, right?

Meyers laughed a little and said, "We are. And yes, I suppose that might be a slight deviation from the norm."

"You bet it is! Anyway, I wanted to tell you that the nurse that delivered the blood sample spoke to me earlier. She told me what was going on down there — about how this Bateman kid is suspected of murder."

"Three of them to be exact."

"I understand there were three victims, Captain. I wanted to express my concern with what we found. I have the report sitting on the fax machine now, and will be sending it as soon as I hang up the phone with you, but Captain, don't be disappointed with what you read. And, just to be clear, I'd like you to know that there is absolutely no way that the results have been fabricated or otherwise tampered with. I analyzed the sample myself . . . personally."

"Okay, doctor. That's fine. I believe our machine is on and full of paper. Send it on. And after everything that has happened around here the last few days, I wouldn't be surprised if you found out that Johnny boy here is with child."

Meyers paused, expecting a laugh that didn't come.

Doctor Morris lingered on the line for a moment then said, "Will do, Captain. But I wanted to tell you one more thing. I have a brother-n-law over here . . ."

Captain Meyers rolled his eyes and thought: *Okay, okay, here it comes.*

". . . he's a senior pharmacist at Tiger Drugs on College Street here in town, and teaches a class at the School of Pharmacy. He knows his stuff. I talked with him a little while ago. He said that Bipferin has some pretty interesting side effects, but they are not that well known or understood by the general public. I assume that you fall into that category, Captain Meyers?"

"I assure you, Doctor, the only drugs I know anything about are aspirin, Excedrin, and the bushel basket of BC powders I have in my desk. Sometimes I even experiment with how all three may affect one particular human all at once, especially after long days of trying to figure out how a deranged teenager managed to kill a camp full of hunters."

Also after long, confusing phone conversations from forensic experts that are slow in making their points.

"I understand your position, Captain, and I don't envy your job at all. I just wanted to make you aware of an interesting coincidence about that drug we found in the armadillo blood. Bipferin is the trade name, but it's chemically known as zolpidem. According to my brother-n-law, this stuff can cause people to do things that reflect the total opposite of their normal personality. I'll give you the example he used to illustrate the effects. Let's say a socially shy fellow somehow winds up at a dance. You see, ordinarily you couldn't force him out onto the dance floor at gunpoint, but if he had been taking this drug, you might find him skipping out onto the hardwood, stripping down to his tighty-whities, and doing the limbo under a flaming bar with a hard on. It's almost as bad as bipolarism. Do you know what that is, Captain?"

"I have some prior experience with that Doctor, from my time over on the Atlanta PD."

"Okay, good. Then you know what people who suffer from this are capable of doing, and then having little or no memory of it later."

"I do."

"Well, to go along with the personality issues, some of the trials with this drug involved sleepwalking or whatever the technical term for it is — except the person seems to be awake. And after they do whatever they do, they have no memory of it."

Meyers butted in. "Let's cut to the chase, Doctor. You all but told me a few minutes ago to expect Bateman's blood report to be clean. Did I misunderstand?"

"You didn't. The sample was a clean as a whistle. But there is one blood sample from a player in all this that we haven't checked, and in my opinion, it might be the most important one to your case."

"I'm not sure who that would be. Maybe you and I both need to be stuck by the —"

Before Meyers could finish the sarcastic remark, Doctor Morris said, "The deer's blood, Captain. We haven't checked the deer's blood."

Meyers was stunned into silence. It was as if he could not even begin to process such useless information. In another moment, he laughed boisterously into the phone.

Through the broken laughter, Dr. Morris said, "Captain, I'm sending you the Bateman's sample report as we speak, and I'm working on retrieving the clinical trials. When I get them, I'm sending them to you to see for yourself what kind of side effects the drug causes. I strongly urge you to take a close look at them. I know it sounds absurd to think that a deer might have been dosed with some drug out in the boondocks of south Alabama, but then again, no one would have expected to find that stuff in an armadillo either. As strange as things seem to be, I believe it's worth some thought and at least a second look.

"Oh, and one last thing. My brother-n-law said that the chemical gives off a distinctive odor when moistened. Supposed to smell like citrus — oranges, lemons, or maybe even grapefruit, especially when it's crushed into a powder. Just thought you might want to know, just in case you run into something that smells funny. Good luck with your investigation, Captain."

Meyers was still giggling to himself, getting over the absurdity, when Deputy Williams stepped over to the fax machine and pulled the report. He glanced at it quickly while he walked to Meyers' desk. "Looks like his blood is clean. I guess that just makes him a bona fide psychopath, instead of just a druggie, huh?"

Meyers snatched the papers from his hand and started reading. When finished, he flipped the first page over and read something handwritten on the second page. It said, "Drug trials on the way, stand by."

Meyers went back to the first page and he quickly scanned the report again, before tossing it haphazardly onto his neatly organized desk. He said, "Oh well, guess he wasn't pregnant after all. The Batemans and whoever they thought knocked him up can call off the wedding."

Deputy Williams smiled as Captain Meyers sat back down and pulled the pack of Marlboros from his shirt breast pocket. A cigarette appeared in his hands, and he leaned back, and propped his feet on his desk while he fished around for the book of matches in his pants pocket. Finding it, he tore out a match, but before he struck it, the fax machine started warming up again.

When the last page came through the deputy handed them to the Captain. It was a horrible thing to have to read. The scientific mumbo-jumbo, and all the confusing graphs and tables made his head hurt. He was on the third page when he saw that a paragraph was circled.

BIPFERIN usage was generally successful at treating short term insomnia and excessive anxiety, with ninety-four percent (94%) of the patients studied experiencing symptom relief. Four percent (4%) showed no effect, while two percent (2%-not statistically significant) suffered from adverse side effects. Those patients experienced moderate to severe mind and mood altering episodes where they deviated from normal behavior of their personality. Also, four percent (4%) of patients experienced lucid sleepwalking, unaware afterwards they were performing everyday tasks and routines while semiconscious. Three (3) patients that suffered from both the mind altering and sleepwalking episodes exhibited severe personality deviations, bordering on minor bipolar tendencies . . .

He stared blankly at the report. Was this Doctor Morris really serious about what he said at the end of their conversation, or was he living in a fairy tale world over at Auburn? Sure, in a cartoon, this could explain everything. He imagined Wile E. Coyote taking little capsules apart and sprinkling the inner goodies over a big pile of bird seed on the yellow line of a remote desert road for the Road-Runner. His mind easily produced the dialogue that poor Wile E. was saying to himself as he worked: *I might not be able to catch that stupid feathered bastard, but if he'll just stop and nibble on this stuff, he'll wake up in an oven on a platter surrounded by carrots and potatoes.*

The veteran investigator just couldn't let himself believe it. This was no cartoon. The three corpses lying on slabs in the morgue weren't a fairy tale. This, unfortunately, was reality, and reality didn't produce deer that could walk into drug stores and pick up prescription medication.

He dropped the report on top of John's clean blood test on his desk, and glancing at it again, he noticed a small detail that he'd missed earlier printed harmlessly between the lines on the transmittal sheet — the 'From' line. The report had not come from the forensics lab at Auburn. It was from the Gateway Inn, St. Louis Missouri. "Clay Bateman," Meyers said out loud. He turned to say something to Deputy Williams, when he heard the fax machine come to life once again. The first sheet came through, and this time it was clear that whatever followed was coming from the Auburn Forensics Laboratory. It was another drug report, and it matched the one sitting on his desk perfectly.

Chapter 6

Pencil between teeth, the veteran investigator carefully read both reports. Side by side on his desk he flipped through each, patiently digesting each word. If it had just come from Bateman, he would have thought that the boy's father might have fabricated the information. He could not believe his eyes, but both reports were identical, and appeared to be legitimate.

He was almost finished when he flipped by an extra sheet transmitted from St. Louis. The final page of the fax was a handwritten note from Clay Bateman.

Jonas: It is my understanding that you don't believe my son is telling the truth about this rogue deer business. Believe me, I didn't either at first. Well, I've found something here that might be of interest to you and the case. At your earliest convenience, please call me here at the hotel. The number is on the fax cover sheet. Sincerely, Clayton Bateman

He picked up the receiver, and reminding himself of the number from the front page, he banged away with a ridged finger into the face of the phone. After a few relays around the front desk at the Gateway Inn, he finally was on the line with the elder Bateman.

"Good afternoon Captain Meyers. I trust you have had a good day thus far?"

"I suppose. The fax note, Clay. Let's cut to the chase here. What's happening up there on your end? What could you possibly have that would interest me and this case?"

Clay held the line briefly, shuffling through a handful of papers on his nightstand. "Jonas, I didn't realize that me coming out here was going to end up helping you and John, but I have been working on something that I think will."

Meyers was waiting for the punchline. *There's nothing in St. Louis that would be helpful (or hurtful for that matter) in a triple homicide case all the way down here in Jessup County!*

Clay said, "I was sent out here to do a little investigating myself. Seems that we had several cases of drugs go missing in the last couple of weeks, two cases of Bipferin were among them. I believe that was the drug you all found in the armadillo blood from my boy's shirt and arrow. And if you took the time to read that information I sent you, you'll see that it is completely plausible that such side effects may cause, shall we say, erratic behavior in a dosed deer."

Meyers huffed. "I don't think —"

"No, I don't think *you* understand Captain. I'm in the process of backtracking the shipments, and I'm getting close to closing the loop. I've got every person I could raise working on it as we speak. If it wasn't for this blasted New Year's Holiday, I'd have everyone in my district on it. Still, we're getting close, and I'm positive that we'll figure out exactly what happened maybe as early as close of business, today. I can't be sure right this second, but it's looking like an inside job."

Meyers skeptically listened to the rant. He was sure that all of it was a dead end. A wild goose chase designed to cast doubt on John's involvement. After all, Clay was the kid's father. He would do anything to make sure John's life wasn't ruined by this. As ridiculous as it sounded, Meyers was becoming intrigued. He wanted to see how Clay was going to do it. What could he possibly come up with out there that would expunge John from suspicion. Who could he pin it on? He quickly ran through the players, but nobody jumped out at him.

"Well, Clay. I'm waiting. Who are you going to run up the river to try to save your boy?"

Meyers listened to a blank line for a long moment, before the phone nearly exploded. Clayton Bateman yelled, "I thought you were an investigator. Didn't you go to school for this stuff?"

The Captain's ego shattered like a dropped pane of glass. He squirmed in his chair trying to think of the next volley of insults when Clay Bateman turned the screws even deeper into his flesh. "Aren't you forgetting something, Captain Meyers? Aren't you forgetting that Kirby McNeil worked for me?"

The line was silent again. Meyers sat frozen in his chair — of all the excuses and scenarios that had briefly ran through his head, he hadn't expected that. Clay Bateman was going to try to sink a dead man.

Clay finally broke the silence, "Now that I have your attention, you need to know one more thing. You are rapidly ascending my shit list, and aren't too terribly far from the top. If you can't pull your head out of your anus for two seconds and at least acknowledge the fact that Kirby may have stolen the drug, ground it up, and dosed some corn or something, and baited the deer on Al's place, then I'll personally make sure that Sheriff Butters busts you down to county road kill collector — with no hope for parole. So keep your *DAMN* phone lines clear and your *DAMN* fax machine on, and I'll let you know when I and my folks nail down exactly what happened with the drug shipment."

The phone made a heavy click, then went dead.

Stunned, Meyers slowly placed the handset on the cradle. He mumbled under his breath, and reached for a pencil and the new notepad waiting for him there on the corner of his desk. He wrote down the particulars of the conversation, specifically documenting how abrasive Clay had been. Once the notes were made, he slipped back into investigator mode, and jotted down the new information regarding the case. Kirby stealing drugs? If so, he must have been working on developing a market for it somewhere. But why would he waste some of it on wildlife, when he could push all of it on the street? Maybe he was testing it, but if it was pharmaceuticals, he would have known the stuff was good. It must have a pretty significant street value. If he was going to risk everything, why would he throw even a small portion away on an armadillo?

Then the more likely solution flashed in his mind. Why not frame a dead employee? Clay wanted to save his smart aleck kid from being destroyed by a drug and murder charge. If he could make it look like Kirby had stolen the drugs and somehow went crazy — that would cast a tall shadow of doubt on John's involvement. That just might be enough to acquit him. Clay Bateman was influential; a favorite son of Jessup County that was friends with judges, legislators, and other big-wigs in Montgomery. If anyone could do it, he could. A shadow of doubt. That was all he needed. The right donation to the right re-election campaign, the right words whispered into the right ears at just the right time, and John would walk. That was it. That had to be it. He was going to destroy a dead man's reputation to save his son.

Meyers shook his head and continued writing. If the conversation with Clay Bateman was as he suspected, a ruse, then he was going to make sure to charge him with aggravated assault and obstruction of justice. He was reaching for his coffee mug, satisfied with the prospect of justified retaliation, when he noticed the fax machine starting up again.

Captain Meyers retrieved the transmission. *If we keep this up, we are going to have to requisition a new fax machine. This one is going to be worn out by the end of the day.*

Sitting at his desk, he carefully scanned through another report from Doctor Morris at the Forensics Lab. He read it once, then twice, and still he didn't understand. Who had ordered what he was reading? And what was the analysis reporting on? Even back in Atlanta he'd never had a day with so many unanswered questions. He took a sip of coffee, hoping the fresh influx of caffeine would help his brain piece it together. The new report was apparently for some sample of livestock feed — a corn-sorghum mixture, and the burlap sacks it was stored in. At the bottom was what looked to Meyers to be a summary of the report. It clearly read: *"The chemical ZOLPIDEM was found in significant amounts on the loose grain and the fibers of the burlap."*

Captain Meyers, fresh off the threatening conversation with Clay Bateman, was smoldering. It was his investigation — he was the lead. Where and what had this analysis come from? He looked back at the report, and two more questions arose, almost as an afterthought: What loose grain? And what burlap sacks?

Meyers turned in his chair and through the glass window of his office, he scanned the open room. Five deputies usually worked the day shift and constantly complained of being overworked and under paid. Meyers saw no one at their desks, in the in the room, or the hallway. There was not a single uniform in sight, much less doing work. A wicked thought materialized. *We'll just have to see just how overworked and underpaid these guys really are.*

He crushed out a half-smoked cigarette, stood, cleared his throat, and screamed: "If anyone can hear me, what's this new forensic report about? Loose grain? Burlap sacks? What the hell is going on here? Why wasn't I notified about this?"

Deputy Ricky Jones ran through the door of the break room. Meyers finally had a target, and slung the loose papers down on his desk. "Please tell me, Deputy — do you know anything about this report?"

Deputy Jones said more to himself than to Meyers, "What report are you talking about?"

Meyers pointed to the papers on his desk, "The new forensic reports on some kind of grain and the burlap sacks it was in, you twit. And I would appreciate it if you'd follow up statements directed to me with SIR. I'm still your superior."

The deputy cautiously said, "I'm sorry, SIR. Deputy Williams must not have told you, SIR."

Veins suddenly materialized on Meyers' neck, and in a forced calm voice, he said slowly through clinched teeth, "No, Deputy Jones, I suspect that since I don't have a clue as to the significance of this, clearly I wasn't thought important enough to be kept in the loop. Do you have any information that might help me understand where this report came from? And if you say the Auburn Forensics Lab, so help me, I'll have you busted down to county road kill collector before your shift is over."

Deputy Jones swallowed hard. "No, sir, I mean yes, sir. I do know where this came from, sir. I, well, we — Deputies Williams, and Brooks, and myself, sir — we were going through the vehicles that came in from the hunting camp. We found something sir. There were burlap sacks in the back of that white suburban. They were folded up and hidden under the spare tire. We noticed something on them when we got them clear. It was a white chalky powder. Being we suspected some kind of drug situation, with the Bateman kid, well, we figured that it might be cocaine or heroin or something. Andy said that it might be the key to the case — something that might explain how he went loco enough to kill the others. We looked for you, but you were out. I believe it was just before lunch. Even tried you on the radio, sir."

Meyers rocked back into his chair, halfway through his slow burn. He quickly replayed the morning activities. That was about the time he was feeding his face at Giggy's. The excuse was legitimate. Maddening, but legitimate.

"Well, Deputy, who gave the order to have the bags and that white powder analyzed?"

"The Sheriff did, sir. He was in his office and we told him about it. We processed and bagged it for him, and he took it over to Auburn himself. He said that he knew the director over there and —"

Sheriff Butters' voice suddenly boomed over his shoulder. "At ease, Deputy Jones." The deputy backed away to one side, almost cowering, and Butters strolled through the door, and tossed the Captain a brown object. It landed in the middle of his desk, rearranging the newly organized papers into disarray. Meyers picked it up, and carefully unfolded it while the Sheriff spoke.

"I think you have been riding these boys a tad hard here lately, haven't you, Jonas? I mean, they can't hardly do their jobs without you jumping down their throats." The Sheriff turned to Deputy Jones and winked. "And a fine job they are doing too, before I forget it."

Meyers looked from Butters to the large brown burlap sack he now held, unfolded in his hands. Printed in the center was: Junior's Alabama Royal New Potatoes. Grown and Packaged by Rickenbacker Farms, Foley, AL 36535. Net Weight 100 lbs.

Sheriff Butters glanced at Jones, who looked like he did not know what to do or what to say. "I suspect the report beat me back? Is that right, Deputy?"

"Barely, sir."

"Good. I do appreciate your attempts at explaining the situation here to Captain Meyers. Excellent work, son. Now what I need you to do is to go out to the parking lot and stall Detective Triplett. I saw his cruiser top the hill behind me when I was pulling in."

"What? I mean, how do I do that, sir?"

"I don't know. Why don't you tell him you are interested in working for him in Montgomery? That usually gets those Bureau boys started easily enough. I bet he keeps a handful of applications in his glove box — ask him for one and a pen. I only need a few minutes here with my number two man to remind him what his job is." He cut a cold eye at Meyers. "And all three of us know it isn't ignoring hard evidence, and riding the deputies too hard."

Smiling, Deputy Jones issued a hearty "yes sir," and hurried out of the room.

The Sheriff leaned against the door frame and shook his head "I think this case is starting to get the best of you, Jonas. I get that you are frustrated. The rest of us are too. Heck, I think Williams spent half the morning drawing up bylaws for the club we are thinking about starting." The Sheriff chuckled lightly at his own joke. "We've had some real honey-drippers before, but I don't remember any of them getting under your skin quite as bad as this one. A little advice for some time down the road. Kick the trashcan, throw your hat, or go out into the parking lot and scream or cuss. Do whatever you have to do to stay sane without breaking something, particularly a fist or foot, but there's no need to tear into the deputies for every little thing that irritates you. Good deputies are hard to find, and God knows they are worth twice what we can pay them. Why do you think I give them a pretty relaxed lead on time and leave? If you run these guys off, how are we going to get everything done around here?"

Meyers wanted to defend his actions. He wanted to tell the Sheriff that he'd been working the leads as best he could, but had been sidetracked, thinking that Clay

Bateman was trying to frame Kirby, to save his kid. He tried to speak but the Sheriff cut him off.

"Do me a favor, and take a deep breath. If you are on edge now, what I'm about to tell you is liable to flip you all the way over. You missed something, and don't feel bad, because it wasn't just you. I didn't see it either."

Captain Meyers opened his mouth, but Butters raised his hand, stopping him.

"Quit trying to talk your way into or out of whatever you were thinking of and just listen to me for a second. You need to try real hard to clear your mind of what you know, or what you think you know about this case."

Meyers looked at him dumbly and nodded.

"Did you see what was written on that burlap sack?"

Meyers took a long look again at the dyed insignia on the face of the sack, silently mouthing the words.

"The wife and I make it a point to swing into Rickenbacker's for some fresh produce every July when we spend our week at the beach. As far as I know they are still in business — I hope so anyway. Their regular red-skins are pretty good, but they don't touch their sweet potatoes. They're as good as any I have ever eaten."

Meyers looked confused and nodded blankly at the culinary report his Sheriff offered. *How can this be relevant to the investigation?*

Butters continued. "That bag you're holding is telling us two very important things about this case. First, Ron over at the forensics lab just told us that sometime in the past, it held corn and sorghum dosed heavily with Bipferin. Hmmm. Let's see. Several big burlap bags of grain that deer love to eat at hunting camp? I think we both know what that means. And secondly, it gives us a clue to the owner. The blood tests, the drugs — all of that helps us with the case, but who those bags belonged to — that would be a very useful bit of information to know right about now. Don't you think?"

Meyers held out the burlap studying the graphic and lettering. Hidden behind the bag, the Sheriff asked, "Besides the fact that it was found in his SUV, which doesn't mean too much because it could have been planted there, who in all this mess is or was from Foley?"

Captain Meyers looked as if he was reliving third grade again — a confused kid staring blankly at a puzzle everyone else in the class had solved, but Butter's final clue swung the doors of his mind wide open and a name suddenly came to him.

Meyers scratched his head, unable to believe it. "Kirby?"

The Sheriff smiled and nodded. "Now you've got it! Kirby McNeil was from Foley."

Chapter 7

It hit the veteran investigator like a ton of bricks. How could he have missed that? It was probably a long-shot to have suspected Kirby, mainly because he was dead, but he *was* in pharmaceuticals, and he *did* work with Clay Bateman. He would have a more than just a working knowledge of the many drugs Gulf Pharmaceuticals handled, he would have had access to them, and more importantly he would have been able to direct shipments. Depending on who he winked at, he possibly could have pulled some strings, and misdirected shipping orders. Kirby McNeil might not have been the most obvious choice, given the circumstances, but a good investigator should have at least given that scenario a fair chance.

Meyers had known Kirby, casually, for better than ten years. And although they hadn't been best friends, he did remember him talking about going home to Foley to visit family, and to go fishing with one of his friends that ran a charter out of Orange Beach. The Sheriff was right — Jonas had missed it completely, or perhaps *dismissed* it completely.

While the Sheriff thumbed his way through the new forensic report, Meyer's mind groped for an excuse. The burlap sack and powder residue were the linchpins for putting it all together. If he'd just known about those two things, he would have easily deduced that there was a better than average chance that the animals down there off HWY 223 actually have been drugged. He tried to downplay it, but deep down he was embarrassed. Embarrassed that information and evidence had been clearly building right in front of his crooked nose corroborating the boy's story; yet he had been so stupidly biased against the fairy-tale, he could not force himself to even consider it. The first thing learned in any criminal justice class is that nothing is done for or against the law without motive. What was Kirby's motive? The Bateman kid had nearly asked the same question yesterday when talking to Triplett. Why in the world would anyone go through that much trouble to drug an animal? Nothing about it made sense.

Before the questions stopped making laps through his mind, Deputies Jones and Williams blew through the doorway, followed closely by a confused looking Detective Triplett. Williams was noticeably pale and short of breath. Meyers thought he looked like he might have seen a ghost, which given the all-to-real probability that a drug blinded deer had killed three hunters in his county two days ago, seemed more than reasonable at the moment. Williams extended a trembling hand and handed a small envelope to the Sheriff.

Opening the fold, Butters asked, "What is it, Son?"

"Pictures, sir."

"That's plain to see Deputy." Butters said thumbing through part of them. "May I ask something else then, just for my own clarification? Pictures of WHAT?"

"We — I mean Deputy Jones and myself found a couple of game cameras in the woods while we were out there the other day recovering the bodies. We figured that we'd take them as evidence and see what kind of pictures they took."

Meyers stared at them coldly, a man who had lost all control of his world. "You took those things down even after I told you to leave them alone?"

"Yes sir, Captain. We're sorry about not following orders, but we've only seen cameras like that on the TV hunting shows. When John told us that there was possibly a new state record buck down there on Al's place, well we wanted to see if there were any pictures of him on the game cameras. We dropped the rolls of film off at the drugstore yesterday, and I picked them up a little while ago."

Sheriff Butters flipped through them quickly. Nothing seemed out of the ordinary. There were pictures of does, a couple of smaller bucks, and a few of raccoons and squirrels. Something did finally capture his attention though. One shot was of a fantastically huge buck deer. He stopped and stared at it a moment wide eyed, then flipped through a few more pictures before saying, "Okay, all I see here is normal stuff, that and one helluva buck. But what's got you wired up, Deputy. What am I looking for here?"

"You can see it best in the last picture, sir."

Butters quickly thumbed through them all, and pulled the last one. He held it for a moment, and his easy smile vanished.

Meyers and Triplett saw the reaction and both said almost in unison, "What is it, Sheriff?"

Butters lips became two thin white lines under his nose. "It's the proof that clears the Bateman boy."

"What?"

The Sheriff laid the picture down on Meyers' desk. It clearly framed the forward half of a massive buck deer with wide spreading antlers with extremely tall tines extending upwards off the main beams. There also was the long drop-tine hanging off the left main beam that positively identified the buck from John's description. Meyers and Triplett were so enamored by the size and structure of the head gear, neither saw what Deputy Williams and the Sheriff had alluded to.

Both investigator's initial scans were a bust. The second time around, remembering his training, Meyers divided the photograph into quadrants and then slowly and meticulously took each apart piece by piece. He was still drawing a blank when Triplett said, "Hey . . . what's wrong with his antlers? They look like they're —"

Sheriff Butters finished the sentence for him. "Red!"

Captain Meyers hadn't seen it, but now the bloody red bone poised above the animal's head jumped out at him like a run-away truck. They were as red as any candy apple he had ever seen at the fair. There was no mistaking it. Triplett whistled through his teeth, and Meyers fell back into his chair, totally exasperated. This one picture single handedly wrecked his whole case. So much for winning the detective of the year award.

Detective Triplett shook his head and said, "Hey, don't deer antlers look like this though? I mean, when they grow them back each year, doesn't the fuzzy stuff come off and the bone underneath look a little bloody for a little while?"

Staring straight ahead at the wall, Meyers answered, "Yes, they do, but that fuzzy stuff comes off in early October. It's called velvet. We are about three months overdue for that."

Sheriff Butters leaned on the corner of Meyers' desk and shook his head. "That's blood all right, and I suspect it's human. The tines are covered in it. The Bateman kid was telling the truth after all."

Meyers could not hope to organize all the incredible questions that quickly occupied his brain. What he painfully realized though, was that John Bateman had sat in that little room, in that uncomfortable chair, breathing leftovers of his Marlboros, and told that story not once, not twice, but three times, and the good Captain had not believed a syllable. And then there was all the Bipferin evidence that came in today, suggesting that the buck had indeed been drugged. The Sheriff was right. John Bateman wasn't lying about what he had barely lived through, and as hard as it was to accept, there still was a lingering question that no one had answered. Why would anyone waste good sellable drugs on some buck deer? Captain Meyers chased a glance at Triplett, then at Butters, and posed that very question.

***

After lunch, the lack of sleep finally caught up with John Bateman. He laid on the hard cot and quickly dozed, but sleep didn't come easily. He tossed and turned, drifting back and forth numerous times across the threshold of consciousness, before he finally succumbed. Thirty minutes into the best sleep he had in two days, a door slam woke him coming from up the hallway towards the offices. He stretched and tried to get comfortable again, when he heard mumblings drifting down the corridor.

John rubbed his eyes, concentrated on the sounds, and realized what he was hearing were conversations. He had not seen Sheriff Butters put the picture of the buck on the table, but from the abrupt change of inflection and volume of the voices, he knew something important had happened. John stood and walked to the edge of the cell and strained his ears. Meyers,' Triplett's, and even Sheriff Butters' voices streamed down the hallway, a crescendo of odd statements — something about bloody antlers. The clear but disturbed voice of Captain Jonas Meyers rushed down the hall, forming the very question that John knew the answer to.

It was time to be heard, and to be certain of it, he yelled, "It's a new state record! That buck is going to hit the record book for Alabama, and probably be in the top five for the world! The drug is a sedative . . . it was supposed to make him easier to kill!"

***

All three men glanced down the hall towards the holding cell. John's voice had come through as loud and clear as the weekly emergency tests that blared from the top of the fire house every Wednesday at noon, but none of them wanted to believe it. If what John had said was true, that meant the top criminal investigator in the county, and one of the best from the Bureau in Montgomery had missed the motive completely. Even Sheriff Butters, who had managed to piece together the possibility that the missing drugs could have indeed ended up in Jessup County via John or Kirby McNeil, had yet to postulate the reasoning behind it. It was just too unbelievably simple.

Illegal drugs were something that Jessup County's finest were accustomed to dealing with almost on a daily basis. In fact, other than a few cases of domestic violence, prostitution, poaching, and other misdemeanors and petty theft each year, the majority of Jessup County's criminal justice activity stemmed either directly or indirectly from people trying to escape the boredom of a rural county by chemically recreating. Drug use and the occasional overdose were terrible, of course, but the main impact it had on the town and county was the desperation seen from the users. Drug money in poor, rural counties was simply a product of addicts scavenging and stealing from others in order to fund their habit, and after years of dealing with the 'normal' drug cycle, it seemed utterly ridiculous to suggest that it might be used in a manner other than strictly human use. Not even Nostradamus could have predicted it.

Triplett said almost laughing, "I don't think I've ever seen anything like this before. Do you mean to tell me that a fellow will go through this much trouble, stealing drugs from a big pharmaceutical company with all the risk that comes with that, just to drug and possibly kill a big deer?"

Still dumbstruck, no one answered.

After a moment, Meyers scratched his head and said, "As bad as I hate to admit it, that's sure what it looks like. Killing a world record buck deer would send you straight to the top in the outdoor and sportsman media and circles. Might even land you a TV show. But I still can't believe it. I suppose Doctor Morris was right when he said that we needed to test one more individual."

Butters and Triplett both looked at him, puzzled, and while Meyers was explaining, the fax machine came to life again. Deputy Jones retrieved the transmission, then walked it over to Captain Meyers and pointed at the name from the cover sheet. Meyers stopped mid-sentence. The fax was from The Gateway Inn.

"What is it, Jonas?" Butters asked.

"It's from Clay Bateman. He was working on trying to find out who had misdirected the drugs up in St. Louis."

Meyers handed the papers to Triplett, who quickly scanned them, before handing them to the Sheriff.

Butters read it, then nodded and smiled. "The cover page here only has the fax number. Do you have the phone number out there?"

Meyers nodded.

"Well get to dialing then. I can't imagine what frame of mind they've been in, but I am sure that he and Layla would appreciate a call. Tell them what we believe has happened, and that their son is no longer a person of interest in this case." He turned to Deputy Williams, who was still standing there with the same dumb look on his face Meyers had. "The kid's clothes are folded on one of my office chairs, Andy. He's probably not going to like the patch job the missus did on them, but at least they are clean. While he's changing, get him a Coke or something, then bring him in here. Looks like we've got some apologizing to do."

Sheriff Butters cut his eyes back to the bewildered investigators. Detective Triplett was tearing pages from his notebook and balling them up into little crumpled spheres and tossing them at the trashcan, and Captain Meyers, who looked like a kid who was playing Clue for the first time (and losing), was shuffling through the papers on his desk searching for the phone number. Both men could not hide the look of defeat.

The Sheriff rubbed his chin. "Now that we know the whos and whats, there's another matter that needs to be addressed. If there's any of that stuff left, and if the deer are still eating it, we're looking at one helluva public safety hazard down there."

Butters checked his watch. "Gonna be dark in a couple of hours. It'll have to wait until tomorrow, but make sure everyone on the day shift clears whatever they had planned for the morning. We need to be there first thing and have a look-see.

He turned back to Meyers and said, "When you get off the phone with Clay, you might want to try getting in touch with that new game warden. What's that new boy's name? Johnson, Justice? The Department of Natural Resources might be interested in this, since it's is one of their constituents who's apparently guilty of murder. Besides, I suspect that y'all wouldn't mind another gun and set of eyes down there just in case you happen upon him, or he happens upon you. Coordinate with warden what's-his-name and see what you can find. Oh, and take John with you. He knows the place, and I betcha he probably has a good idea of where Kirby might have dumped the bait."

The Sheriff turned to Triplett and said, "And you aren't getting out of this that easy either. Get on the horn with your folks in Montgomery and tell them you are going to be busy in the morning. I don't care what was on the docket, re-schedule it. Now if you all will excuse me, I've got a few phone calls to make myself, and if anyone has any ideas how to break all this to Al's, Renn's, and Kirby's families, not to mention the newspaper, I'll be in my office banging my head against the wall."

Chapter 8

"I appreciate you helping us out this morning, John." Detective Triplett's words were barely audible over the roar of the tires on bad pavement. "I also wish we could have arranged better accommodations for you last night. With your folks still stranded in St. Louis, the Sheriff — well all of us for that matter — thought that it would be better for you to stay with one of us. I hope that motel room was at least bearable."

John said nothing, but did manage a subtle nod.

Triplett twisted his back to each side a couple of times and said, "It wasn't my bed at home, but the proprietors of the Jupiter Inn didn't spare the pocketbook when they chose bedding arrangements. My mattress passed the test with flying colors. How about yours? It had to be better than that steel frame cot."

The sleepy teenager nodded again, yawned, and checked his watch by the clock in the police cruiser's radio. Triplett followed John's stare and focused briefly on the little blue analog numbers 5:46 glowing in the dark dashboard. The cruiser started to rumble as the tires drifted across the broken white line onto the chipped apron of the highway, and the detective corrected the steering wheel and glanced at the side mirror. He could barely make out the county squad car following closely behind.

Triplett focused again on the highway and thought about the situation. He couldn't blame John for being withdrawn. The poor kid had experienced a lifetime's worth of fear in just three short days. Witnessing the deaths of three good friends, running for his life in the dark woods narrowly escaping death himself, and then being all but accused of crimes that he could not hope to imagine a realistic alibi for — it was a wonder he made it through all of that without blowing a fuse or at least melting a few wires.

Someone who was not aware of the circumstances would have probably thought that John was being excessively rude, but Triplett knew better. Whatever hard feelings this teen harbored, were more than justified. And no amount of coddling or compassion from anyone was ever going to undo what had been done.

Despite his compassion, the detective owed John nothing, professionally speaking. What transpired over the last few stressful days was just a necessary part of the job. But somewhere down deep, there seemed to be something personal between them that needed to be addressed. Triplett hadn't been able to put his finger on it, but after struggling with what to do, and what to say, and how to act around him all morning, the thought, now feeding on his brain like an undiagnosed disease, finally made itself known.

He did owe John something after all. At the very least, he owed him a chance to be friends. Triplett casually tapped along on the steering wheel with the beat of the music coming from the radio, thinking. The only way to chip more of the iceberg away was to show John that he was human too. Even a middle aged law enforcement professional, hardened by dealing with years and years of the worst humanity could dish out had feelings. And those feelings were just as tangible as a high school student, half-way through his senior year.

"Sorry for getting you up this early too." Triplett smiled and tried to laugh. "It seems like we have been apologizing for everything under the sun since yesterday evening, haven't we? I had no choice this morning though. We had to get up early; I've got to be back in Montgomery this morning by eleven o'clock. Court date. If I'm not there preparing to give testimony by then, my boss will cut my throat."

Triplett exhaled a long sigh. "I love my job, and I love fieldwork, but the courtroom is something I could live without. We really go the extra mile out here hunting down the facts and evidence, and then those sleazy defense attorneys do their best to dismantle and discredit us. Heck, sometimes the most air-tight cases are blown or thrown out because those yellow-bellied dogs get paid to muddy up the water on behalf of first-class scumbags. They are very good at — let's say — casting a shadow of doubt."

***

John listened to Triplett extend the olive branch, but he wasn't ready to accept it just yet. He sat still and watched the road ahead of him slowly become more and more obscured by a white foggy mist.

It took a few miles, but eventually John started to feel better. Surprisingly, he found Triplett's conversation, particularly his admitted shortcomings, semi comforting. That, and him tapping out the beat of "Walk this Way" on the steering wheel. Aerosmith was one of his favorite bands. It was probably just a tool to try to get him loosened up, but it didn't matter. John was ready to talk to someone as a regular person, not someone who was on the verge of being accused of murder. But he had something planned for the detective.

John stared straight ahead through the windshield and said, "Do you mind if I ask you a few questions, detective?"

Triplett shook his head while trying to keep the cruiser between the yellow and what was left of the white line.

"Was it just me or was that clock in the interrogation room screwed up?"

Triplett laughed out loud. It was perceptively different than the fake laugh he'd attempted earlier. "It wasn't you. I noticed that too. Sometime during one of those first breaks we took, I asked about it. Captain Meyers said they had it made that way to keep their suspects shook up. Apparently, one of his mentors in Atlanta had one just like it."

He looked at John, still smiling. "Did it work?"

John nodded again. Not wanting to sound too eager, he waited a few minutes before asking the second question. When the timing felt right, he asked, "What you said before about the cases going bad — how many cases like that do you lose?"

The question appeared to pierce the detective through the heart. "What do you mean?" Triplett asked a little too quickly, trying to hide his building anxiousness.

John rephrased it. "How many cases do you lose that you are really supposed to win?"

"Well, technically it's the district attorney that loses, but it's how we do our jobs out here that gives him what he needs to do his. It's the agents that make or break a case, but we are all just spokes inside a big turning wheel. We all work together."

Triplett ran a finger back and forth between his shirt collar and neck a few times before continuing. "But to answer your question, I'm guessing that maybe seven or eight cases out of a hundred have something go wrong, or a witness clams up, or something like that."

John immediately sensed a change in Triplett. He wanted Triplett to admit that sometimes things go wrong, but he had no idea that it would come so quickly. He merely wanted to expose the detective's soft underbelly, and his question did that and more. Now, John was a Great White circling his wounded prey.

The tires clicked musically on cracked asphalt, and there was a slight whistle of wind seeping around one of the back window seals. Enjoying the feeling of control, John thought he saw a bead of sweat form on the detective's forehead. He chose to let the anticipation build — he wanted Triplett to feel as uncomfortable as he felt stuffed in that tiny little interrogation room, and it was working.

Making him wait for it was proving to slowly dismantle the seasoned lawman right there in the car. John held his tongue, and glanced in the side mirror. In it he saw the muted headlights of the following police car through the fog.

The only thing that would make this better is if Captain Meyers were here in the car to help Detective Triplett eat this last question.

The thought made him smile, and abandoning the side mirror, he delivered the coup de grâce. "What about the other way around?"

"Pardon?"

John rephrased the question. "How many cases do you and the DA win that you should have lost?"

***

The question stung him like a nest full of irritated wasps, and the detective's eyes became slits feeling the coldness of John's voice. He knew this wasn't just a simple question, it was outright retaliation. Triplett's face flushed, and the anxiety that John planted with the second question now blossomed into a warm rage.

As angry as he was, Triplett knew better than to explode. He knew as well as John that the question was valid. If John's father hadn't been working on the case, unknowingly, five hundred miles away in Missouri, and if the two deputies had followed directions from Captain Meyers and left those game cameras alone, John could have very well found himself locked away in a state penitentiary awaiting trial for three counts of capital murder. And to top it all off, he likely would have had no chance of acquittal. The best that he could have hoped for in such a scenario was to plead insanity or admit to being on drugs, then spend the rest of his life trying to dig out from under that burden. What a way *not* to finish up your senior year of high school.

Triplett quickly regained his composure. He silently reassured himself that the system did indeed work. He had seen the wheels of justice roll across case after strange case, and always the truth was revealed some way or another. Sometimes those wheels turned slowly, but they kept moving, perpetually forward, towards the truth, the whole truth, and nothing but the truth. There had always been exceptions though; cases that didn't quite add up, and yet the accused still went up the river. He feared that John's case would have been like this. And given the two painful questions, he knew that John knew it too. Triplett wiped a few beads of sweat from his forehead. *The file and what I first thought about this kid was right. He's exceptionally keen — smarter than some lawyers I know. He knows what to say and more importantly when to say it. If he ever abandons journalism as a career, any law school would be lucky to have him.*

Triplett came back to John's question and focused all of his energy on deriving an answer. "I dunno, John. I can't see there being too many though. The criminal justice system has too many checks and balances to make many mistakes."

It was the best he could do at the moment. He did not mention them, but he was aware of two examples of just what John asked about. The first one was a rape case that was re-opened and thrown out of court some five years later due to a change in forensic technology. And the second was a convenience store robbery in Birmingham where a teenage kid from the wrong side of the tracks was found holding a smoking gun when the police responded to the silent alarm. The clerk was dead, and even though several people were outside when the gunshots rang out, there were no eye-witnesses to the murder. The kid confessed to the robbery, but said he did not kill the clerk. The surveillance cameras in the store were not working properly, and had only shown broken images of the suspect in the store, but not holding a gun until after the alleged time of the murder. No one saw anyone else leave the place between the shooting and when the police arrived minutes later. It was his word against the State's, and the choppy video's that he was the only perpetrator. Several years after the conviction, a witness came forward and admitted seeing a second suspect running from the side entrance just after the gunshots started.

Both times, the evidence at the moment pointed towards the wrong people. But still, the wrongs had been righted; it just took a couple of small retrograde revolutions by those heavy wheels of Justice before moving on. Detective Triplett dealt with it as best he could; it wasn't his, or the DA's fault that those things had happened. It was out of their control. That is what he told himself anyway.

John seemed disappointed with Triplett's paper-thin answers, and if he had any more questions, he chose not to ask them. He simply said while staring out the window, "I suppose you're right. But when it nearly happens to you, I guess it really starts to sink in that things like this happen. Infrequently or not."

Triplett knew that the kid needed and perhaps deserved better answers, but at the moment, there was nothing more he could say to make it better. He frowned thinking about what he should have said, and what he could say now to try to change the subject. The answer was right there in front of his face . . . the blinding fog.

Triplett said, "This dang soup seems to be getting worse. How much further to the hunting land John?"

"Oh, about three more miles."

"If only I didn't have to be back in Montgomery — I can't see a thing past twenty paces."

John shuttered, and Triplett caught the movement out of the corner of his eye and understood. He asked the only thing he could ask. "Are you okay?"

"Yeah — it's a little spooky." The kid's voice quivered slightly, and he pushed up his sleeve checking his watch. "Should've been light enough to see thirty minutes ago. It's still pretty dark out there."

Detective Triplett could hear the worry in John's voice, and although his vindictive mind immediately came up with several sharp comments of his own, he decided to let it go. "Well, if you don't feel up to joining us, and I don't blame you if you don't, just point us in the right direction and we'll try to find those bait sites. I think you were right when you suggested that Kirby probably was dumping that stuff near his stands. If we can find them, we should be able to find the corn, that is, if there's any left."

The road straightened and the fog seemed to dissipate. Triplett increased the speed from barely over thirty miles per hour to nearly fifty. The detective relaxed his grip on the steering wheel, paying a little less attention to the road and a little more attention on John. He was impressed at how John kept it together throughout the ordeal, but as they neared the place where he witnessed such atrocities and literally faced his own death, the kid's silence seemed to scream panic. The transformation was not subtle. The stoic high school student who withstood the intense interrogation like a hardened mastermind now looked like a frightened child.

Triplett mind worked quickly, trying to come up with something to ease John's anxiety. "You know, John, I think what you are doing with your writing is really neat. I never could write much, but I did enjoy American Lit in high school and college. I even liked a little poetry. There was one that I always liked the best. I had it memorized for a while, but can only do bits and pieces of it now. Tennyson. Have you ever heard of him?"

John nodded his head.

"The one I liked the most is "The Charge of the Light Brigade." He wrote it about a famous mounted charge on a line of artillery in a battle that the Brits were involved in a long time ago." Detective Triplett smiled. "You'll probably get into it in college next year. There's a lot of good stuff to read out there — the classics — and your freshman and sophomore years of college are usually when you get a chance to read them. Out of all of the ones I read, Tennyson was my favorite. That one in particular is a dandy. I think I can remember part of it still." Triplett rubbed his forehead with his free hand, trying to remember. "I don't think this is in order; just bits and pieces, but here goes.

Half a league, half a league, half a league onward.
Forward, the light brigade. Charge for the guns he said.
Into the valley of death rode the six hundred."

The detective hoped for some kind of response. After a moment, he realized that he wasn't going to get one.

"There was another part of it that was not quite as inspiring. Tennyson suggested that the soldiers knew that somebody had made a mistake, because nobody in their right mind would order light cavalry to charge a line of artillery. Let's see.

Theirs not to make reply. Theirs not to reason why.
Theirs but to do and die. Into the valley of death rode the six hundred."

Triplett shook his head, whistling through his teeth. "You know he never said how many of them died, but it must have been quite a few because he mentioned that horse and hero fell, and when they rode out of the valley he phrased it: 'but not the six hundred.' Ole Tennyson really did a number on that one. Never understood how a poem could be an uplifting example of heroism, and at the same time, reflect such tragedy. Guess that's what so cool about writing, huh?"

John smiled, and Triplett was relieved to know that he had finally found some common ground with this kid. Feeling good about it, he asked, "I saw from your file that you're pretty much going to write your own ticket through school and into the workforce, being a wordsmith and all. What made you decide to be a writer?"

Before John could answer, the cruiser banked into a curve, and suddenly the fog was back, thicker than before. Triplett redirected his attention to the road, and slid his right foot from the accelerator to the brake. He gently pressed, just enough to feel the car respond, then released the pedal, content to coast. Halfway through the curve, something suddenly materialized in front of them. It was big and brown and right in the middle of their lane. The startled detective jammed the brakes, but it was too late.

Chapter 9

Deputy Andy Williams followed closely behind Triplett's cruiser. Since they left the parking lot at the Sheriff's office, both patrol cars, weathered Crown Victorias, pushed forward through the thick fog like a pair of submarines cutting a hole through the sea. Deputy Jones, still not over last evening's adventures in billiards and beer at The Wagon Wheel bar was snoring in the backseat, but Williams and Meyers were very much awake. Neither had spoken for several miles, both concentrating on keeping the car in the road. Up ahead, the tail lights from Triplett's state cruiser faded into and out of sight. They could have been connected to a dimmer switch, controlled by a mischievous child.

Williams adjusted his hands on the wheel, and without blinking said, "Can you see their tail lights?"

"Not right this second." It wasn't the superficial question that caused him to be short. It was the infernal fog, as thick as he'd ever seen. There were stretches of it that made seeing the hood ornament just a few feet in front of the windshield a challenge. The combination of keeping his deputy behind the wheel focused on the highway, and mentally reviewing their task for the morning were slowly tearing his nerves apart. He was still having a hard time believing what had apparently transpired in the woods down here, but he knew that the possibility of coming face to face with a rampaging buck strung out on some crazy drug in this cloak of mist was far from ideal. Leave it to a prima donna from the Bureau to force them to go before the fog had a chance to lift.

Meyers hid his concern well from the deputy. He was able to pass everything off as just another day on the job, but deep down he was worried. He'd look at the road for a while, then study the county road map for a while — anything to take his mind off what may be waiting for them when they struck out into the woods. He ran a finger along a line on the map. It was leading towards the red circle John had drawn in, marking the entrance to the Rutledge property.

Meyers said, "There should be a slow left turn in about a quarter of a mile, then there will be a little over a mile of straight road. After that, there'll be a curve to the right. The entrance John told us about is a few hundred yards past that curve."

The tail lights from Detective Triplett's cruiser came back into view. They were just faint pink dots, staring back at them through the muck.

"Be careful now," Meyers said. "They are closer than you think. We just had breakfast a little while ago and I'm still full, so there's no need to eat up the back of that Ford just yet."

As quickly as they had appeared, the two lights again faded out of sight. Deputy Williams craned his neck and cinched down harder on the wheel. "You know Captain, we really could have used a few more folks down here helping us. How many men did Natural Resources say they had in the search over at Eufaula?"

Captain Meyers rolled his eyes. It was the second time Williams had asked that since leaving Halifax. The deputy's raw nerves were starting to show, and the

Captain knew that a few years immersed in Atlanta's Peachtree District would cure him of a lot of that foolishness. "They said they had ten boats on the water, all carrying two man teams. And from what I could gather from the conversation, I think that 'search and rescue' has officially turned into just 'hope of recovery.' It's a damn shame the weather's been warm the last few days. If it was a normal winter, it would have been too cold for them to be out on the lake like that. You know, the Mayor down there claims it's a New Year's tradition — something like a red-neck polar bear club. But they wuss out if it's really cold. Some years they've waited until March to do it."

Meyers felt the road level, coming out of the curve. Following along on the map, they now had a straight stretch of road in front of them, at least for a little while. They could also see Detective Triplett's taillights well; the fog seemed to be lifting. That was good news. Williams exhaled a sigh and said, "I've never heard of anything like that happening to a boat motor. Did they say whether it was an outboard or an inboard?"

"They didn't." Meyers coolly lit a cigarette, and cracked the window, tossing the spent match. "What I'm really wondering is if they had the balls to ask the Mayor for a breathalyzer? He was supposedly at the wheel when it happened. I don't know if I buy that a half-submerged log could damage the engine enough to compromise the steering, but still allow full throttle. I think the better explanation is that all of them had four, or five, or fifteen too many toddies at brunch, before they got on the water. You know, working up the nerve. From what I gather, they were on the upper end of the lake too. Not very many people are skiing up there during the summer when the lake is at full pool, let alone during the winter drawdown. I can see that crowd down there now, half lit or better, daring one another to slalom through the stump beds."

"Yeah," Deputy Williams said, "I get up on that end bass fishing a couple of times each spring. I can't imagine trying to water ski through that mess. The river channel would be the only place you wouldn't be likely to hit anything, and it's mighty narrow that far up the lake. And sometimes it's not what you can see that'll get you. I've hit some serious downed logs hiding just under the surface in the channel before. Nearly threw me right out of the boat."

Meyers nodded. "Well, we can't be sure of what they were doing or thinking, but I'm absolutely certain of one thing. A skier bear-hugging a solid, six-foot high cypress stump running full blast will more than get the job done. Supposed to have made one heckuva pop when he hit, too. They said it sounded like somebody hitting a sheet of plywood with a baseball bat."

The cruiser picked up speed, traveling down the straight stretch of road, and the fog continued to dissipate. What once was a thick soup was now a thin broth, and both men could plainly see the rear of Triplett's car some sixty yards ahead.

Deputy Williams continued to talk about this and that, but Meyers drifted away on his own thoughts.

It was the broken promise he made to himself the evening before that still hurt. The drug reports and the game camera film turned everything he thought he knew about the case completely upside down. He nearly missed two turns on the way home from work, as he kept churning through the new information, and what it meant. When he walked through the front door, his wife,

Rachel, met him with a kiss, and quickly sat him down to some of her blue ribbon meatloaf, but even then, Jonas Meyers didn't feel like eating. He managed a few bites, but soon found his way to the living room where a few beers and the evening news waited for him.

He told himself over and over not to worry over the mistake any longer. What was done was done — what had happened had happened. It was all in the past, and nothing he could do would allow him to go back and change anything. There was a problem though. Every good detective knows that a big mistake like that, if allowed, would eat away at a person's mind. It can turn an otherwise productive investigator into a blubbering mass of useless flesh. Meyers knew he was quickly approaching that dreaded state.

He sat in his recliner and sipped on a beer, while the news anchor started the broadcast with breaking news out of Eufaula. Five boaters were stranded for three hours on the lake earlier that day due to a boating accident. A rescue party found the stranded boat at dusk, but one skier remained missing. The Mayor of Eufaula was on board but had not made himself available to the media.

Mentally and physically exhausted, Meyers hit the mute button, and closed his eyes. Two beers later, he kissed Rachel on the cheek and told her he was turning in early, and after a soothing shower, he slipped between the sheets. It was well past 3:00 a.m. when he finally slept, but when the alarm clock sounded just an hour and a half later, the thoughts and images of Al, Renn, Kirby, John, and of course, John's pet deer were all there again waiting patiently for him to return to the land of consciousness.

It was probably delirium from the lack of sleep, but while brushing his teeth in the pale yellow glow of the bathroom light, he caught himself smiling in the mirror. The smile quickly turned in to laughter, and Rachel rolled over and stared at him from the bed. She said that there was absolutely nothing that could be that funny this early in the morning. Not a fan of early mornings either, Captain Meyers ordinarily would have agreed without protest, but this morning, something *was* that funny. Kirby thought he had it all figured out. He was certain that he'd wind up the sportsman of the year in Jessup County, heck, probably the whole state. They would invite him to retell the story at the Birmingham and Montgomery annual deer expositions, and probably interview him on the news. His face and the buck's would be all over the local papers, and national magazines. The overbearing irony of it all was utterly laughable. Never before in the history of man has a plan backfired so disastrously.

Even now in the car, with Deputy Williams going on and on with a lot of nothingness about bass fishing in Lake Eufaula, and Deputy Jones snoring in the backseat, Meyers could only smile at what happened. Yet somewhere stuffed beneath that smile, were still bleeding wounds. If he had of just known about the sacks, the grain, and the analysis — it would have been a different story. It would have been plain to him then.

The justification was comforting, but not for long. Even with the potato sacks being from Foley, clearly pointing a sharp finger towards Kirby, John would have been the obvious choice. Whether he admitted it or not, a pharmaceutical rep's son could have easily accessed the drugs, and being a freelance writer, it wasn't totally insane to think that he wanted, or more likely, needed to drug the deer. He needed to have new and fresh material to write about, and killing a state record deer with primitive archery tackle would have been the ultimate win-win. Any of those magazines would have begged for a story like that, and probably paid dearly for it.

But something else was slowly gnawing at Captain Meyers. He had not made a mistake like that in years, and wasn't happy about being shown up about it. Well, it really wasn't a mistake just yet. It was really an omission — an omission that probably would have sent an innocent boy to prison for many, many years. Meyers frowned. Arguing semantics with himself was useless, but that was exactly what he was doing. Mistake or omission, the difference between the two was minimal when it came to a young man's life. It didn't feel good to be called out like that, but there was a bit of comfort in how it all happened. At least the correction had come from his own Sheriff, and not that hot-shot from Montgomery. The wheels of justice had been brought back quickly to the right groove, thanks to Sheriff Butters . . . and Clay Bateman.

Deputy Williams gazed through the windshield and saw the end of the straightaway. Triplett's cruiser banked then was gone, cloaked again by the fog, and in an instant their own car was engulfed again in the blinding whiteness. The road, what little could be seen, started to turn and Williams gripped the wheel tightly and began to brake. Meyers strained his eyes, but could only see ten paces of road in front of them, while the rest of the world seemed to be blotted from existence. Williams braked harder, and Meyers turned just in time to see him consciously blinking, as if it was somehow going to magically clear his field of vision.

There are times when the blink of an eye can cause a person to miss things they needed or wanted to see, a baseball player trying to hit a fastball, or a child trying to see a shooting star, or perhaps a bolt of lightning during a summer storm. However, Deputy Williams' hard blink caused him to miss a split second of reaction time. The road, completely clear just before the final blink, afterwards was filled with 3600 pounds of metal and fiberglass on wheels. Meyers instantly grabbed the dashboard, while two glaring red tail lights flashed brightly in his eyes. Williams desperately snatched the steering wheel to the left, and pounded the brake pedal, trying to avoid the collision.

Somehow in that abbreviated reaction time, the deputy's quick reflexes had been nearly supernatural. The Crown Victoria managed to turn somewhat to the left and slow considerably just before their right headlight plowed into Triplett's left tail light. In the bone-jarring impact, Triplett's cruiser was forced into a tight clockwise spin, stopping just short of completing a three-sixty, while the county cruiser's rear end lifted and spun into the opposite lane, facing back towards Halifax. In less time it took for Deputy Williams to blink, both cars, badly wounded, had come to a screeching halt.

Meyers and Williams sat there nearly hyperventilating. They looked at each other, symbolically nodded that they were all right, then turned their heads towards the backseat where Deputy Jones was laying in the floor, moaning. The hungover deputy looked like a scattered pile of windblown leaves. He raised his head, blinked a few times, and Meyers saw a bad gash open above his right eye. He took a deep breath, and quickly looked away.

Trying not to pass out, the Captain focused on Triplett's vehicle that they now were oddly facing. Meyers saw that Triplett and John were both moving. and blankly rubbed the back of his neck trying to retrace what went wrong, he was reaching for the seatbelt when he heard something on the road emitting a sickening guttural moaning sound of something in pain — then it all slowly started to make sense.

Wild boar? Deer? Bobcat? In rural south Alabama, it could have been any number of things darting out into the road in front of them. The thought lingered, and then sudden shrill screams started coming from the other vehicle. A surge of adrenaline hit the Captain, and he punched at the seatbelt, banged on the door a couple of times with his shoulder, and was out.

Chapter 10

For a brief moment, John and Detective Triplett stood in the road, staring at what they hit. Lying on the pavement was a man wearing a shredded brown hunting jacket that looked like it had gone through a sausage grinder. Everything from small cuts to deep jagged lacerations were scattered on his hands, face, and neck, and the outside edge of his left nostril was ripped clean from his face. All that was bad, but his right leg was the big problem. Just above the knee, or where his knee should have been, a jagged piece of bone protruded through a large ripped hole in his jeans.

John heard the county cruiser's door open. He looked up and saw Deputy Williams limping over. "What in God's name did you . . ." He stopped, looking. "Holy Shit, it was somebody!"

Williams frantically looked around. "Where's Captain Meyers?"

Triplett stepped back, clearing the line of sight, and the deputy saw his Captain lying on his side on the pavement, out cold.

"I saw him jump out of the car, but didn't see him go down. Jeeze, looks like we have two victims instead of one."

John leaned and gingerly thumbed away a ribbon of blood flowing into the man's eye. *The car couldn't have done all this. This poor guy looks to have just gone the distance with a heavyweight contender. There's not an inch of him showing that isn't cut, bruised or swollen.*

As they gawped, the man's sickening moans stopped. Bloodshot eyes opened and saw the small audience hovering. The man tried to speak, and on the third try, sound finally came from his throat, faint, almost a whisper. "John — John Bateman." The man turned his head, and spit a dark stream of blood along with several pieces of what looked like bits of tooth from his mouth, then looked back up at the group. "I should have known you'd be the one who'd kill me."

Williams and Triplett looked at one another before turning to John. The shaken teenager looked as shocked as they did. They said almost in unison, "Do you know who this is?"

Before John could muster a response, the cracking voice came again. "Sure he knows me. He knew my niece too. Knew her all too well, and it ended up getting her killed."

John went down to a knee. "Donnie! Is that you?"

"It was me. I'm not exactly sure who or what I am now though."

Donnie Abernathy tried to move, but nothing seemed to work, either from injury or overbearing pain. Finally his right arm came free, and went to his face. Trembling fingers quickly found a large tear on his lower lip, and several bad cuts on his chin and cheek. Crawling fingers smeared fresh blood across his face, giving the appearance of some ancient Apache war chief ready for battle. Quivering, the arm moved again, this time sliding down his chest and right thigh until he found what everyone except Meyers was looking at. Those same trembling fingers gently touched the jagged end of his femur.

Donnie body flinched and he tried to raise his head. "Sonuvabitch! What happened to my leg?"

Detective Triplett grabbed his hand and pulled it away from the wound. "Don't do that. Don't try to move. Your leg's broke, and it won't do you a bit of good to see it right now. It's not that bad, so just lie back and try to relax."

It was a lie, and everyone, including Donnie, knew it. The wounded man rested his head again on the pavement, while he moaned a howl of torture. Sucking in a deep breath, he adjusted his upper body, but when he moved, his thigh above the fracture also moved, and a stream of red fluid suddenly spewed in an arc several feet above the open wound. A new look of sick fear flashed across their faces.

This time it was Williams who screamed. "Oh my God — it's an artery."

For a silent second, all anyone could do was watch the copious spurts of red leave Donnie's leg each time his heart pumped. John could feel his legs buckling under him, and he turned in time to see a pale Detective Triplett go down on his hands and knees. The detective frantically crawled to the edge of the road, heaved twice, and vomited. Deputy Williams's countenance was frozen in sheer panic, and Captain Meyers still lay sprawled and unconscious a few paces away.

With nothing in his stomach left to purge, Detective Triplett wiped the spittle from his lips and said, "We need a tourniquet."

Immediately, Deputy Williams was out of his uniform, and was tugging at his plain white undershirt. Once off, a keen blade quickly shredded the white cotton into long strips, starting at the neck-line, and extending to the shirttail.

John was not medically trained, but he did have something working to his advantage that the others lacked. He had just spent three months immersed in Anatomy and Physiology class at school. Trying to calm himself, he surveyed the wound again, and realized what the deputy was planning. "Wait a minute," he said, "I don't think it's bad enough to shut the leg off completely."

Williams yelled back, "Wait? We don't have time to wait for nothing. This man is going to bleed to death if we don't hurry up and do something."

John reached out nearly touching the bloody wound at Donnie's knee. "Yeah, but I don't think it's the femoral."

Williams ignored him and continued to construct the makeshift tourniquet.

"No, really! We learned about this in school — it's not enough blood. The femoral is one of the biggest arteries in the body, and it moves a ton of blood. If it was cut, we'd be swimming in it. There are several other smaller arteries in that area, like the popliteal. It still isn't good, but as long as it's not the femoral, we have options."

Detective Triplett watched John make his point, and then looked at Williams who was fishing the strip of fabric under the leg just above the jagged wound. He brought both loose ends up and tied a couple of overhand knots, snugging it up against Donnie's ripped blue jeans. He was reaching for his billy club to twist the loop to tighten it when Triplett grabbed his arm.

"Would you listen to this boy for a minute! I know what I said, and what you're thinking, but there's no need for him to lose the leg if we can help it."

John quickly and coolly said, "The femoral moves about a pint and a half per minute." John glanced at his watch, calculating. "It's been about four minutes since we hit him. If it was the femoral, he'd be more than half out of blood now, and there's no way he'd be conscious." He looked at the streams of red pulsing from the wound, and then up at Donnie's face, still watching everything with those spooky bloodshot eyes. "I know it looks bad, but see how small that stream is. It's really not that much blood."

"So what if it isn't the femoral?" The deputy said. "I don't care what it looks like, he's still losing a lot of blood. We need to do something, and unless you know how to stitch up a leg artery with a pocket knife and shoestrings, a tourniquet is all we got."

A voice came from somewhere behind them. "The boy's right, Andy."

All three turned and saw Deputy Jones staggering towards them, pressing a bloody bandanna against his forehead. "That's not enough blood for the big artery. Now it might just be nicked instead of completely cut, or that close to the knee, it just might be the popliteal."

Detective Triplett backed away from Donnie, making room for Jones. The dazed deputy removed the cloth and touched the laceration above his eye. He muttered to himself something about needing shoestring stitches too, before reapplying the bandanna. He kneeled and gingerly placed two fingers on Donnie's neck. "Pulse is still strong in the carotid. That's always a good sign. Now let's check on that leg."

Jones' motions were deceptively fast and calculated as he pivoted on one foot and took two steps backwards, placing him directly over the injury. He didn't say anything, but hummed a nameless tune as he gently finished tearing the jeans and investigated the wound. He pointed at the leg. "The flesh is nice and warm above and below the knee, but we need to get this thing back close to where it's supposed to be, if nothing else, to make it look better. John, Jeff — hold him steady. Particularly his arms. This is going to hurt like hell, and I don't want that big joker opening up any more gashes on my face while I'm trying to save his life. Andy, get down there with him. Hold his hand and talk to him. No matter what you hear or feel, be sure to maintain eye contact. He probably feels more like a science experiment than anything at the moment, but right now, he needs to feel human."

Deputy Jones then turned to the injured man. He saw beads of sweat forming across his bloody forehead, and those bloodshot eyes still wildly rolled around in their sockets. Jones waved his hand in front of the injured man's face trying to get his attention. "Donnie. Donnie! Look at me Donnie."

The eyes stopped rolling, and seemed to focus on the deputy.

"Very good, Donnie," Jones said in a calming voice. "Now listen to me. We are going to do something here that's gonna help your leg, but it's going to hurt something terrible. I'm going to straighten it out, and get it back into position. I'm not going to try to set it — I'll leave that for the surgeons after we get you to a hospital. I promise you though, it'll be better if we can get it at least pointing the right direction."

He took a deep breath, adjusted his footing, and nodded to John and Detective Triplett. John braced against what at the moment felt like a limp fish. But he knew what was about to come. Whenever Deputy Jones started on that leg, Donnie would become a rampaging wild animal.

Chapter 11

Donnie Abernathy's low moans exploded into shrill screams, hacking through the endless fog. John could barely watch, but once where he only saw concern and worry, he now reeled at a sweat beaded face tormented with excruciating, hellish agony. Even Deputy Williams, who was supposed to be comforting Donnie, looked away as the injured man fought the pain with everything he had. Jones positioned the leg correctly, and with a few quick movements, the jagged bone neatly disappeared under the torn skin and ripped muscle tissue.

"Okay, that was easy enough." The deputy looked pleased with himself. "While you've got him, I'm gonna see if I can figure out what's going on here with all this blood."

Two probing fingers slid into the wound, following the hot pulses of blood. Much like pressing a thumb over the end of a water-hose, the extra pressure caused a spray, and instantly, Jones's uniform turned red. He shielded his eyes with his free hand, and continued, sinking his fingers past the first knuckle, then the second. The deputy's hand was halfway in the wound, and Donnie was screaming again, when a smile broke across his face. "Ah ha. Got you, you little sucker!"

Deputy Williams yelled, "What is it? What have you got?"

"It's not the femoral. It feels fine. What we are looking at is that smaller artery down around his knee, or where his knee used to be."

Amazed, John softly said, "So it was the Popliteal!"

Jones repositioned his hand in the wound. "Bingo! That's what it is, all right." He smiled at John. "Whatever you made on your last anatomy test, the teacher needs to double it."

Deputy Jones continued to explore the wound, and Donnie screamed and squirmed uncomfortably under him. "I think that's bone fragments I'm feeling all around it. That and part of what I think is the patella — the knee-cap. It must have shattered when that bumper hit it, and a shard of bone or something must've got to the artery. It's not severed clean. Feels more like a pretty good nick. I don't think it's that bad, but I think I'm going to have to keep pressure on it until we can get him somewhere."

Jones adjusted his fingers again, and the flow of blood immediately stopped. It was like a surgeon had clamped the damaged artery. Everyone blew a collective sigh of relief, and Deputy Williams reluctantly slid the billy club back into the slot in his belt. Pointing to the strip of cloth still tied around Donnie's leg, he said, "Are you sure we aren't going to need this?" But before anyone could answer, he realized the futility, and asked three more questions that were more relevant. "Where we going to take him? And how are we going to get there? Don't you suppose we need to get on the radio and get an ambulance or a helicopter headed this way?"

"Helicopter is what we need, but I don't think it's going to get clearance in all this dang fog." Deputy Jones closed his eyes and slowly ran his free hand across his face.

Quickly, the decisions were made. "Okay, here's what we'll do. I'm going to sit right here and keep pressure on this artery. Andy, get on the radio, call the office, and tell Sheriff Butters what's happened. Tell him we think we have the patient stabilized, but could be missing something, so speed is important. Tell him to call Montgomery and get either a chopper or ambulance on the way to Halifax — and I mean five minutes ago. We'll meet them there.

"John, I want you to wake up Captain Meyers." He glanced at the Captain, still out cold on the pavement. "He's been out long enough — it's time for him to get in the game. We're going to need everyone we've got to get him in the car."

John looked back and forth between Jones and Triplett. "How do I wake him up?"

The deputy said, "Shake him, slap him . . . whatever it takes. Just get him up. If you need it, there's a large bottle of water in the backseat of our cruiser I was using to treat my hangover. Get it and splash him a few times in the face, then hit him in the head with the bottle. Hard."

***

John and Deputy Williams both started their tasks, leaving Triplett still holding one of Donnie's arms, getting a closer look at the wounds. There was no way the car could have made all those small cuts and gouges. In all the excitement and focus on the leg fracture, no one thought to ask Donnie what happened to him, and why he was standing in the middle of the road on a hopelessly foggy morning.

Detective Triplett said, "Hey Donnie, can you hear me?" Donnie Abernathy swallowed hard and nodded. "Okay, Donnie, my name is Detective Jeff Triplett. I hate to tell you this, but I'm the guy that hit you with the car. I didn't see you in time. Probably not much comfort in it, but I'm sorry about that."

Donnie blinked and whispered, "If I make it out of here alive, and still have two legs under me, I'll be sure to kick your ass."

Triplett wasn't sure if Donnie meant it as a joke or not. He smiled anyway. "Let me ask you something. What in the world were you doing in the middle of the road? I just took a look at your injuries up here around your face and neck. You're beat up pretty bad. I don't think the car did all this. What happened to you?"

Donnie's voice was fading. "It was a deer, a big ass buck deer. He ran me down in the woods this morning."

"A deer did this to you?"

The wounded man tried to nod. "Crazy, bastard bout' near killed me too, and then you came along and finished me off. Never . . . saw . . . either . . . of . . . you . . . coming."

"You hunting alone this morning? Are there any others out here with you?"

"Was . . . only . . . me." Donnie's eyes closed and his head limply rolled away from him.

"Donnie? Donnie!" Triplett started to panic, and gently slapped him on the cheeks.

Jones said, "Don't worry. I've still got a healthy pulse. He just passed out, probably from the pain."

***

When everything was set, Triplett, Williams, and John, heaved Donnie Abernathy, with Jones still applying pressure to the artery, into the backseat of the county cruiser. Williams climbed into the front seat in time for Sheriff Butter's call back on the radio. The signal was weak, but they were able to communicate. Butters told Williams that the pilot said that the fog was thin enough between Montgomery and Halifax to make the trip, so a helicopter was being prepped for airlift. Flight time was going to be twenty, maybe twenty-five minutes, and that they'd have the bird in the air ASAP. Butters suggested the landing zone be in one of his pastures right off HWY 223, a half mile south of town. They could land right beside the highway. He and anyone else he could get to drive a squad car were going to be there, lights flashing, marking the landing zone for the chopper.

Williams keyed the mic, "10-4, Sheriff. We have Donnie in the car and are in route now." He glanced in the rearview mirror and saw Jones nod, answering his silent question.

The engine fired, and the Crown Victoria disappeared back into the fog. The last thing they saw was sparks flying from the dragging bumper, then there was nothing but a silent county road, engulfed by an uncomfortable cloak of heavy mist. John, Meyers, and Triplett stood in the quiet, staring blankly at a large circle of Donnie Abernathy's blood on the ragged asphalt.

Chapter 12

"Dispatch, this is JC-102."

Miss Judy, sitting behind that sliding window at the Sheriff's office, responded almost immediately. "Read you JC-102."

"Dispatch, please contact JC-100."

Captain Meyers hardly had enough time to release the mic, when the Sheriff's gruff voice came through the speaker. "Read you Jonas. I'm glad you called. I was about to get on the horn with folks up in Montgomery to see what I needed to do to try to contact y'all. I didn't know if we could talk directly with the state car or not."

"10-4, JC-100. The radio is standard issue, just like the Troopers have. I can switch bands from UHF to VHF to talk to our dispatch or the state folks. Be advised, JC-100, we are en route to the Rutledge property. We are still a go to look for the baiting sites."

"10-4. Y'all need to watch your backs out there. A call came in from the Privette place ten minutes ago. Luther Privette's boy went out this morning to go to work and found the front end of his truck worked over. They said they pulled what looked like a twelve-inch deer antler out of the radiator. Now I know Luther and the bottle aren't strangers, but I don't have any reason *not* to believe him. He's been hunting deer for forty years — he knows what a deer antler looks like, drunk or sober."

The transmission stopped, and a brief wave of light static filled the air. Meyers adjusted a knob and regained contact with the Sheriff, still talking. "The Privette place is less than a mile from Al's, and I believe they have a common property line. It sounds like maybe that buck — or maybe another one — is still at it, and has started to whip up on anything it takes a notion to, living or not. We've got to find out how much of that laced bait is left down there if we can. If I could send anyone else down there, I would, but right now, I've got to make sure that chopper finds us. I don't think this blasted fog is getting any worse up here, but it sure as hell ain't getting any better. For now, you're on your own. Do what you can, but be careful."

"10-4 JC-100, copy."

"One more thing." The sheriff's voice resonated again from the radio. "Remember, I promised Clay we wouldn't make John do anything he didn't want to do. So after he shows you where to go, you leave him right there in the car. It's fine if he wants to go, but don't force him."

"10-4."

"Roger, Jonas. Let me know what y'all find. When the bird leaves with Donnie, we'll be on our way."

Chapter 13

The county cruiser rumbled along on bad pavement; its twin headlights stabbed through the muck, illuminating what might have been only thirty feet of blacktop. From the backseat John peered out the window. Landmarks were barely visible, but he was able to profile the hazy outline of the double red gates that kept Jarvis Keeting's herd of Angus Cattle out of the road. And just past that, he saw the pastureland turn into a towering wall of timber. It was Rutledge timber, and he knew they were getting close. John directed the detective, pointing ahead and to the right, marking where the turn-off would be. The entrance came into view, and brakes squealed as the car slowed then bounced and creaked, making the transition from flat county road to the unimproved two-track leading into the woods.

"Tell me something, Captain Meyers," the detective said, holding firmly to the steering wheel. "I've never seen anyone handle a medical emergency as well as Deputy Jones did back there. Looked like he walked straight out of a hospital ER. He's bound to have had some kind of medical training somewhere."

"Yeah, he used to be in the National Guard. I think he was in a medical unit. I remember seeing it on his resume when he applied to the Sheriff's office. You know he's really a pretty smart guy. I think he did college on the GI Bill. Then he applied to Medical School, was accepted, but jumped ship after the first semester." Meyers shrugged his shoulders. "I've done a bunch of things that I've regretted in my time, but none of them even comes close to quitting on something as potentially lucrative as a medical degree. I asked him one time about it, and he laughed it off saying it just wasn't for him.

Detective Triplett shook his head, his voice trailing off. "All that aptitude, thrown right out the window . . . what a waste."

"He's better than most you'll see around here. I believe he moon-lights as an EMT or an ambulance driver or something down in Dothan when he's not being one of Jessup County's finest."

The conversation faded between them, and in the backseat John peered blankly into the gloom. A hint of terror started to grow inside him; it was the same feeling he had sitting in the tree three nights ago, listening to a maniac buck circle beneath him. Watching them draw up the plan back at the Sheriff's office was easy enough — they were all safe there. But bouncing along on the woods road, only a furlong away from where the murders had been committed, and he himself had only been a whisper away from being ripped to shreds, John was second guessing everything, as sweat began to sluice down his face, and wild thoughts once again pried their way into his mind.

The car rolled to a stop in the dead-end parking area. It was maybe twice as wide as the woods road they drove in on, suitable for only two vehicles if parked carefully. Triplett shut the engine off, and they sat there in the half-light, listening to the hot engine tick. John stared out the window, and the woods around him seemed to pulse and flex menacingly, slowly closing in around the car.

Captain Meyers lit a cigarette, took a deep drag, and said a little too cheerfully. "Well gents, looks like this is the end of the line for mechanization. It's strictly heel and toe from here on."

Standing at the front of the car, Detective Triplett and Captain Meyers watched as John opened Triplett's small notebook and laid it on the hood. In the quiet, they could hear the gentle flow of Indian Mound Creek, some forty yards ahead of them, protected from sight by the fog and the enormity of the timber. John visualized the tract and started making a map on one of the pages. To their right, the creek ran for a hundred yards before crossing over onto Privette land, and to their left, upstream and to the west, the channel covered almost three-quarters of a mile on Rutledge property, before crossing County Road 112 at a little steel bridge, near the camp house.

With unsteady hands, John drew the county road on the page, and then more carefully drew a straight line off of it, then a small circle that he accentuated with a bold dot in the middle. "Here is where we are right now." On the side of that small circle, he started a dotted line moving left across the paper. After drawing an inch or two of line, he stopped and looked up, pointing at the edge of the woods at a small opening, barely visible in the fog. "It's hard to see it, but that's the main trail that carries you across the place. It's fairly straight, but there are a few twists and turns here and there. Nothing that'll get you turned around though. It's parallel with the creek all the way across, and nearly cuts the place in two; half north of the creek, and half south."

He returned to the notebook and drew a gently swaying solid line across the entire page following alongside the dotted line, signifying the creek, then John continued making the dotted line farther to the left. At the end of the main trail, John drew a small circle. Then he drew in four trails branching off the main trail, two on the upper side of the dotted line and two on the lower side. At the end of each line, he drew a small circle. He tapped the point of the pen on one of the circles. "These are the food plots. We have two above the creek and two below the creek. And of course, you see the one at the end of the main trail."

Both men nodded.

"Dad had a couple of stands in the woods along the creek. But Al and the others always liked to hunt around the food plots. If I'm guessing right, Kirby would have spread the bait close to stands that were already in place. Anyway," John said coming back to the point, "if you just stick to the trails, you should be able to get to all the locations worth looking at. The trails are self-explanatory, and there's really no way to get lost. The main trail, for the most part, goes straight in and comes straight out. It dead ends at the last food plot. Where each smaller trail breaks off the main one going to the food plots, there are signs posted on trees telling you which field lies at the end. Dad and Al made it simple, they just numbered them. Field one, field two, three . . ."

Captain Meyers repeated the instructions. "No loops, no cut-throughs, just a few twists and turns along the main trail that itself dead ends in food plot number five? And if you break off the main trail, you go to only one of the first four food plots that will be numbered by a sign where you turn off the main trail? And there is only the main trail in and out, no other way to get out of here?"

John's forehead wrinkled, as he pointed at the map. "Well, the only thing you'll really have to pay attention to is if you turn right or left off the main trail going to a food plot. Because if you turn right onto a trail to go to a food plot going in, when you come back out to the main trail, you'll have to turn right to continue west. That means you have to turn left to come back to the car. But if you turn left off the main trail to go to a field, when you come back to it, you'll turn left to continue west on the main trail, and right to come back here. Just keep your eyes open for the field markers and keep up with yourselves on the map."

Captain Meyers said, "Sounds easy enough."

John numbered the food plots on the map and put a star on the second and fifth ones. "We usually didn't swap hunting spots, and these two were Kirby's favorites. I'd try these first."

"Thanks, John," Detective Triplett said. He took the notebook from John and looked over the rudimentary map. "I know you heard Sheriff Butters while ago on the radio. I wasn't going to do it, but since we're down two men, I've got to ask. We need all the sensory we can muster out there. I'm not going to force you to go, but I'd like for you to consider it." The detective stared at him, thinking. "I'll tell you what. I've got something for you." Captain Meyers' eyes widened as the detective leaned down and pulled up his pants leg. Instantly, he palmed a Smith and Wesson snub-nose revolver. He pressed a small lever on the side of the frame, and the cylinder swung free, exposing the shiny brass cartridges. "There are five .38 rounds in the cylinder, and I have nearly a full box of ammo in the car here. I assume from your background you have a pretty good idea how to handle a handgun. It's yours if you'll help us."

Triplett waited for a response that didn't come. He spoke again; this time no one could deny the gravity of his pleas. "Look, you explained it all perfectly, and the map is great, but that doesn't replace actual knowledge of the lay of the land. I don't know what it would take for you to feel good about this? Is there anything else I can say? Anything else I can offer?" He cut an eye to Captain Meyers looking for support. "The Captain and I really need you out there with us."

Besides fielding John's acidic questions on the way down from Halifax, all morning the detective had radiated nothing but calculated coolness. But now, the chinks in his armor were becoming visible. "John, I don't like the idea of what might be waiting for us out there, but it's my job. It's how I earn my paycheck. I don't want to put you in danger, but I could do my job better, and more efficiently with your help."

Triplett's eyes begged, but John still said nothing. The teen dipped his head and stared at the tops of his boots. John noticed that his own legs were quivering. Guilt, terror, shame, fright, and a multitude of other emotions were all there in a big way, and they were all crashing his system, all at once.

John said with tears starting to form in the corner of his eyes, "Didn't you two see those pictures from the morgue?"

"Yes we did," Detective Triplett said still holding John firm in his stare.

"I just don't see why you have to do it? I mean, there can't be that much of that stuff left out there. They are going to run out sooner or —"

Captain Meyers interrupted. "You're right, John, we could do that. But you heard what Sheriff Butters said while ago about the Privette boy's truck. We aren't dealing with a closed system here. If we leave everything alone and just hope that the problem goes away, we might be coming back down here this afternoon or tomorrow or the next day with the coroner stuffing and shuffling more body bags. That buck nearly killed Donnie just this morning . . . didn't he?"

John was screaming on the inside, but nothing made it past his lips. It was quiet there in that opening, and the murmurings of Indian Mound Creek once again dominated. Somewhere downstream, a lone crow cawed twice from a treetop. Triplett and Meyers stood there watching and waiting for John's final decision. He at last gathered himself and said, "I can't do it. I'm not going back out there."

Chapter 14

"There's nothing to it," Triplett said, bobbing a finger at the car radio. "I've got you on the right band and channel to hit either county dispatch, or Sheriff Butters when you key the mic. All you have to do is press the button and start talking."

John looked at the mic in his hand and the radio itself, bolted to the console. "What if I can't get them?"

"If no one answers you right away, give it ten or fifteen seconds and try it again. After five or six tries like that, if nobody answers, then you can just switch the bands and you can talk to my folks in Montgomery."

While Triplett showed John how to switch radio bands, Captain Meyers walked to the passenger side and pulled a sawed-off Remington 870 pump shotgun from the backseat. He'd taken it from the county cruiser before Williams left for Halifax. He worked the action, chambering a shell from the magazine, then reached into the floorboard and produced a beat-up box of buckshot. Turning it over, seven shells fell into his hand, and he tossed the empty box into the backseat. Three shells went into each of his pants pockets, and he held the last one for a moment — admiring bright red plastic and shiny brass between thumb and index finger. John looked up and noticed him smiling. Meyers worked the action again on the shotgun, but didn't cycle it completely. It was just enough to eject the round in the chamber. He slid that round into a pocket, and placed the seventh round from the box back into the shotgun's chamber. "Lucky number seven, don't fail me now," he said, slamming the slide forward, and double checking the safety.

John turned back to Triplett just in time to catch the last bit of instruction on the radio. He repeated the steps back to him out loud, effectively passing radio training, and then the detective handed him a small handheld two-way walkie-talkie. Triplett keyed the mic and suddenly a blaring stream of squelch filled the air. The detective backed up several steps to clear the distortion, and lightly whistled into the receiver. John's radio copied the test.

Triplett put a hand on John's shoulder. "I don't blame you for not wanting to go. When you described what happened down here it sent chills down my spine. And at the time, I wasn't even sure how much of it was real. Truth is, I'm not really getting a warm and fuzzy about going out there, but like I was telling you in the car, it's my job, and my boss and the Sheriff too, expects me and Captain Meyers to do our best work at all times. We are supposed to serve and protect, and that's exactly what we intend to do."

The detective lifted his pants leg and adjusted small leg holster. John looked down and caught a glimpse of the small revolver. For just a second, he thought about going with them. But his inner voice quickly came to life: *Don't even think about it. You are not the one getting paid here.*

Triplett situated his pants, then pursed his lips. "It's probably best that someone stay here at the car anyway. It's always good to have someone manning the radio . . . just in case." He reached for John's left arm and looked at his watch. 6:33. Triplett pushed up his sleeve, pressed a few buttons, and made an adjustment to his own watch.

"Okay, we're synchronized. We're going to do this Army Ranger style, just like your dad would. I'll check in with you on the hand-held every five minutes starting at 6:40. If for some reason I don't —"

Captain Meyers butted in again. His voice registered equal amounts concern and uneasiness. "If he or I don't call you within thirty seconds of our check-in time, just get on that damn radio and tell the Sheriff to bring everybody he can. And bring them right now."

The two men checked their side arms, and double checked their loaded clips, then nodded to each other a sign of unspoken readiness, and started for the woods. John pressed the mic on his walkie-talkie for one last check. He thought about Tennyson, and wanted to say, into the valley of death rode the six hundred, but he didn't. Instead he simply said, "Test — one — two." Triplett gave him a thumbs-up as he and Captain Meyers disappeared into the mist.

***

John sat in the front seat of the Crown Victoria, taking turns staring at his watch and the walkie-talkie Triplett gave him. It was a solid half-mile to that last field, and he had walked it many times before. But all those times trekking the trail, he had never once timed it. Just like the strange backwards clock in the interrogation room back at the Sheriff's Office, not having a reliable time-line was beginning to worry him.

Where are they now? A brisk walk will get you three, maybe four miles per hour. But in this soup, and being cautious to boot, they'd probably be lucky to make two. How long is this going to take?

John looked around for something to write on and with. There wasn't so much as a used napkin in the entire car, and the pencil he found in the ashtray had no point.

Hey, I don't need anything to help me figure this out. Hmmm — let's see. It's about a half-mile to that last field. If they are making two miles in an hour, a fourth that distance should make a fourth of the time. And a fourth of an hour is fifteen minutes.

John's arithmetic was correct. As long as Meyers and Triplett didn't stop for anything, they should make the last field at 6:48, and he thought he'd give them a couple of minutes just to be kind. At least now there was a loose timeline, and he almost laughed, thinking that he might look closely at the possibility of majoring in logic next year in college.

Detective Triplett broke the silence promptly at 6:40. John had never been so happy to hear someone's voice. The second check came through five minutes after that, and the third check, too, was right on schedule. At 6:54, the radio came to life again, and John noticed that the detective's voice was nearly a whisper as he spoke. "All right John, we're still on the trail, but we can see field #5 up ahead. Where do we need to go from here?"

"That one is long and skinny, running away from you. Kirby's stand should be on the left side, maybe a little less than half way across."

Two minutes passed.

"Okay, we found it. Let's see, I've got 6:56 and 40 seconds. Are you registering the same time?"

John's watch was running one second behind. "Close enough."

"Just consider this one the 7:00 check. Will start to search for bait, and get back with you at 7:05."

"Okay"

Triplett called promptly at the 7:05 and 7:10 checks. John was starting to feel better. They had been in the woods for a long time, and hadn't mentioned anything about any deer, or anything else out of the ordinary. Maybe the bait had run out after all?

At 7:14 Detective Triplett once again keyed the mic. "Hey John, we got a bait site. It was about seventy yards from the stand out in the edge of the field. It looks about done. Just a few ground up kernels scattered about. Nothing left here to worry about. We're headed back to the number-two field now."

The 7:20 check went smoothly, and at 7:25, the radio came to life again. "We're here at the number two field. Captain Meyers says we are standing next to a big white oak tree where the trail empties into it. Which way do we go from here?"

"You should be close to it. Supposed to be on the right side of the trail, across from that white oak. If you get out into the field, you've gone too far."

There was a pause. "Got it. Thanks."

At 7:29, Triplett's voice again came through the small speaker, still whispering. "We've found another bait pile. There's a good bit of corn left on the ground too. Don't know if it's spiked or not, but Captain Meyers says it smells like lemons. Will advise on the next radio check."

John looked at his watch just as the analog registered 7:35. The walkie-talkie was silent. Triplett had not been late yet with a report, at least not until now. John's heart began to race.

Five seconds over.

Ten seconds over.

Twenty seconds over.

John felt his palms damp as he reached for the car's radio.

Chapter 15

In the stillness the buck quietly fed. He nibbled at the mass of yellow kernels, raising his head occasionally, surveying as much as the field as he could still see. His eyes were almost useless now, clouded over by some foreign, sticky film, but as nature always commands he still heeded natural instincts. Even if the matter wasn't afflicting his eyes, the fog would have greatly reduced even his visibility. The heavy mist seemed to flow around his movements as if he were swimming, and while he chewed, the moisture from the air made his mouth wet. It tasted better than the water that stood in the long, flowing pool he was accustomed to drinking from, but almost anything tasted better than that. The kernels were filling him, and the emptiness he felt inside his belly slowly waned. It was a good feeling, and one his small, primitive brain could easily understand.

As far as deer go, he was an exceptional specimen. He had always been able to hear better, or see better, or sense things better than others. Even his brain seemed to be just a bit quicker processing the information his eyes, ears, and nose provided. It was his gift, and with that glorious gift came life. Now, with the animal's eyesight strangely impaired, something had changed. It was difficult to understand, if a deer's mind could understand such things, but his other senses seemed enhanced, somehow trying to compensate for that shortfall. The new sensory thresholds he now possessed were just short of supernatural. The animal felt strangely connected to his surroundings, as if he was actually a living, breathing part of the environment. This mighty buck didn't just stand on the ground, he was part of the earth. He just didn't breathe the air, he, like the fog, was a ghostly mist, free to flow with the wind as casually as any speck of dust might ride the currents on a windy spring day. Without trying, he simply *felt* what was going on around him, like a spider perched in the middle of his web might feel for vibrations from an unfortunate insect.

It was with these new heightened senses he suddenly felt something, almost as subtle as a slight change in air temperature, or even air pressure. The tingling sensation told him something was coming — what yet, he could not tell. He stopped chewing, and raised his head high. The crushed yellow kernels overwhelmed his tongue, and the strange tartness that accompanied it still coated the insides of his nostrils. They were useless. Above his head though, two sensitive ears twitched and turned, changing their aspect to the world, probing incomprehensible depths for the cause of the feeling. There was nothing at first, and he chewed again and swallowed. Before he lowered his head for another bite, both ears magically detected sound.

There it was again. Footsteps. The dampness of the leaves scattered along the ground hid the sounds well, but with each passing moment they grew louder. Whatever it was approached quickly, and for a brief instant the animal showed signs of nervousness. Instinct again prevailed, and both lungs began loading his blood with oxygen, preparing for flight, and that glorious white tail, the trademark of the species, twitched as it began to rise. The working ears continued to capture the footfalls, and his brain finally sent the signal. It told the animal to move.

He crept into a small tangle hidden from view just off the opening. Even with afflicted eyes he could see them now; two upright forms gesturing and communicating, not more than fifty yards away. They continued making those low noises, then they slowly moved back up the trail. He thought they were leaving, but they turned and walked into the woods. Moments later, they were back in the field, this time they were moving back and forth, not covering the same step twice. It was if they were searching for something.

The buck looked again in at the mass of yellow kernels in front of him at the edge of the field, then back at the two figures approaching. The empty feeling in his abdomen was coming back, but the overwhelming desire to stay hidden wouldn't allow him to move back into the open. He didn't want to feed in front of an audience, but the animal's stomach slowly began to override his brain. That primal feeling of irritation that drove him to fight with his own kind for his chance to mate began to grow inside. Although it wasn't exactly the same, the feeling was akin to hatred, and by far was the strongest feeling a male deer ever had. Irritation quickly gave way to the urge to fight, and after watching them for a few more minutes, it escalated to a state of being that was alien to him. He was now feeling the urge to destroy.

The buck's hiding place was ideal. It was close enough for a chance to quickly move and strike, yet not so close he could be easily discovered. It was obvious that whatever they were, they possessed poorer senses than even the worst of his kind, or they would have already known he was there. That would work to his advantage. He could use that to make his stand. They were not going to take his yellow kernels away. They were his, and were going to stay his.

The breeze moved gently, the fog with it, and he lifted his long snout trying to test the air. There was still nothing there but that strange, acidic smell. Understanding that his nose was going to be no help, a pink tongue slipped his lips, tasting the suspended mist. It was no longer the clean sweet taste of pure water. Ruining it was the lingering taste of something bitter and pungent. It was like tasting the putrid black mud from a swine infested river bog. These two could not be that filthy, could they? No matter, he wasn't planning on eating them anyway. He had taken care of their kind before — he knew exactly what to do. When the time was right, he would spring, but for now, he waited.

Chapter 16

Twenty-five seconds over.

John had the radio mic in his hand, and was beginning to press the button, when . . .

KA-BOOM!

The single blast echoed loudly down the creek, and the start almost lifted John completely off the cruiser's bench seat. His eyes bulged, and his heart seemed to lodge in his neck; for that one split second the teenager registered nothing but raw panic. There was no time to gain composure before three more successive shots followed. All four were the unmistakable deep booming reports of the shotgun unloading heavy buckshot rounds. The explosions changed pitch, becoming sharp and choppy. John recognized the change. The pistols were now being used. Four, six, eight explosions thundered down the creek so quickly the panicking teen could scarcely differentiate between individual shots. He could almost hear the metallic clanging of the action cycling the brass rounds.

Then there was silence.

John was paralyzed. He stared blankly at the walkie-talkie urging it to say something, but it remained silent. He waited and watched the radio in his hand, but time was not a luxury he could waste now. He pressed the button, and trying to hide hysteria, said, "Detective Triplett? Captain Meyers? What's happening out there?"

No response.

John tried again, but still no answer. He reached down and fumbled with the car's radio, finally got the transmitter free. "Dispatch, dispatch, this is John Bateman. For God's sake please answer me!"

"This is dispatch, got you John. Go ahead."

John stared at the radio, not really sure what to say. Disjointedly, he finally managed to say, "Gunshots — a lot of em — need help now! Captain Meyers says to send everyone you've got!"

"10-4. The helicopter left Halifax a few minutes ago with Mr. Abernathy, and Sheriff Butters advises they are on the way. Just hold on John, help will be there shortly."

More explosions shook the fog. It was a flurry of pistol fire; three, four, five shots echoed around him. From movies and cop shows, John realized that when a pistol is fired that rapidly, it was usually out of sheer desperation — more so for effect than accuracy. They had to be in trouble, if both were still alive.

He sat there holding the radio, helpless as a newborn child. He stared through the car window at the dark void — the start of the walking trail that Detective Triplett and Captain Meyers disappeared into just over an hour ago. What was happening on the other end of it? John blinked and squinted as the opening in the timber morphed into a big gaping maw; the hungry mouth of the trailhead leading straight into the bowels of his nightmares. He shook off the cruel joke conjured by his imagination, and willed himself back to reality.

John closed his eyes. *They told me what to do, and I did it. Let it be known far and wide that John Bateman did not falter.*

He was right. He relayed the communication breakdown and sounded the distress signal — his sole responsibility. There was nothing to do now but sit and wait. Or was there? He reasoned that two men — two brave men were out there in harm's way doing their jobs, trying to protect the citizens of southern Jessup County, and he was just sitting on his rear end in the car. It was like he was watching a bad movie projected onto the windshield of the Crown Victoria. The plot of the story had taken an unfortunate and unexpected twist, the good guys were in trouble, and the cavalry was probably going to arrive just in time to haul two more bodies out of the Rutledge tract. But what else could he do?

While his eyes remained shut, visions of that bad movie on the windshield transformed into a documentary showing events of the last twenty-four hours. He relived, almost in slow motion, the remarkable actions. Deputy Ricky Jones did the unthinkable with Donnie's leg. Deputy Andy Williams, without any hesitation, constructed a tourniquet out of his t-shirt in order to save Donnie's life, and volunteered to drive back through miles and miles of dangerous choking fog to deliver him into the hands of medical attention. Captain Jonas Meyers sprang from the damaged car immediately after a bone-jarring collision, knowing that he'd swoon at the first sight of blood, and now he and Detective Jefferson Triplett were somewhere out there, going against God only knows what, trying to serve and protect.

If only Dad were here. He'd know what to do.

But Clay Bateman was hundreds of miles away snowed in at the Gateway Inn in St. Louis. Yet even from that far away, Clay still managed to do his part. After wading through pounds and pounds of company records, he discovered that Kirby was the rotten apple. Not only that, he was able to produce the drug trials, proving that there could be side effects transforming an impaired subject squarely into an elaborate fit of mayhem. Then John thought of Joni and Marissa, managing to run Captain Weak Knees out of the room with a joke syringe, and offering to help anyway they could, even offering to fake the blood test.

John opened his eyes, and Detective Triplett's words rushed back to him. 'The Captain and I really need you out there with us.' He smiled at the thought of being needed, but it lasted only a second before a rancid feeling came over him. It was like the detective was there patting him on the back and snidely whispering, 'That's Okay Johnny-boy. Just sit right here where it's safe. It's probably best that someone stays here at the car anyway — just in case. Someone needs to work the radio while the real men are out there doing their jobs.' The phantom words left a bitter taste in his mouth.

Well one thing's for sure. The 'Just in Case' ship has already sailed.

It all came at once, crashing down around him there on the Crown Victoria's stodgy gray seat fabric. It wasn't the embarrassing and giggly facts of life that most kids learn about on the school bus. It was the true facts of life — the real, bold, unselfish, pure sense of duty that drives men and women to do the right thing despite the all too real possibility of injury or death. For the first time in his life, John understood. When it came right down to it, people do what needs doing. It was the unofficial creed of the honorable and descent.

John's guts churned as he realized that stinking drug-crazed animal, which had already killed three of his friends, was likely killing two more good men right now. Where fear and apprehension once lived inside him, a gale of boldness blew. Now through cinched teeth he said out loud, "By God, there *is* something I can do."

John quickly went through the car again. It was clean. No back-up guns under the seat, in the glove box, or anywhere else someone could stash a handgun. If only he had that snub-nose .38. It was almost comical. When Triplett showed it to him before, John thought that it wasn't much of a gun, now if he only had it, it would be enough to take on a hundred maniac deer.

Confidence surging, John envisioned how it would end. The charging deer would come at him hard out of the fog, blowing snot with every breath, those daggerish antlers leading the way. He would stand there waiting, unafraid, then the carefully aimed revolver would spit fire, and a neat little hole would open up between those two demonic eyes, spitting his brain into two mangled pieces. The gun would speak four more times, and the sickening thud of lead smashing against skull would follow each shot. Then it wouldn't be his father, or Triplett, or even Captain Meyers saving the day. It would be John Bateman, standing tall over the beast — execution complete — before another man died

He pressed the button on the walkie-talkie again.

Nothing.

Another gunshot rang out from up the creek. It sounded desperate and lonely. Any lingering thoughts of waiting quickly vaporized when he saw his bow and quiver in the backseat. Maybe it was not a .38 slug smashing into the animal's brain after all. Maybe it was to be the cold stinging steel of a razor-sharp broadhead cleaving the beast's brain in two.

John pulled his bow from the backseat almost as ceremoniously as Meyers had pulled the Remington out earlier. He draped the quiver around his shoulders, and slipped the walkie-talkie into a front pocket in his chamois shirt. He was halfway to the woods, when he remembered something. How were the Sheriff and the others going to find them? John ran back to the car. "Dispatch, dispatch, this is John Bateman again."

This time it wasn't dispatch that answered him. "Sheriff Butters here John. We are about 30 minutes out. What's the situation down there?"

"Not good. I've been listening to gunshots for a little over five minutes now, and I can't raise Captain Meyers or Detective Triplett on the walkie-talkie."

"Okay. Just sit tight. We are coming as fast as this fog will let us."

"That's not going to be good enough. Do you have a piece of paper handy?"

"What? What are you talking about?"

"Do — you — have — a — piece — of — paper?"

"I do, but what do I need it for?"

"I'm about to tell you exactly where to go once you get here."

"No, no, no, son! You sit there and wait for us. Whatever is going on down there, you probably aren't going to be able to help. Those two can take care of themselves. No need for you to start bumbling around in the fray and wind up getting hurt."

"No time. Gotta do something. Are you where you can write?"

John quickly walked him through it, paying particular attention to where the turn off the county road was, where the trail head was, and which field Meyers and Triplett were when all the shooting started. Butters started back through it, repeating the directions, but when he purposefully stumbled, and asked for clarification, John wasn't there.

Butters' frantic voice came through the speaker in vain, "John? John! Dammit boy, you're going to get yourself killed!"

Chapter 17

Somewhere along the trail, John reached and ran right past the point of no return. The dark timber was swallowing up the trail behind him, and turning back to the parking lot and the police cruiser now seemed just as dangerous as forging ahead. Hope has driven many a fool to either fortune of failure, but John wanted neither. What he hoped to find when he spilled into the mouth of the second field were two men holding smoking guns standing over a dead animal. There's always hope he told himself, but the frantic style of shooting just minutes earlier, and the silence from the walkie-talkie suggested differently.

Covering the ground faster now, he tightly gripped the osage bow. A primitive, short range weapon, yes, but a deadly weapon none the less. He probably would have breathed a little easier with something else, but for now it was all he had. It wasn't all bad though. John shot that skinny piece of osage wood well right from the start, and it was deadly on the armadillo at the camp house, and the doe standing in the creek. Now he needed it to work its magic once more, at a time when the stakes were at their highest. With the arrow on the string, he could be at full draw in the blink of an eye. Hopefully a blink was all he needed.

Up ahead he saw the sign marking the trail to second field come clearly into view, and not breaking stride, John swung to the left onto the smaller trail. He covered the hundred and fifty yards quickly, but slowed to a cautious walk when the trail spilled into the field. He was just steps into the opening when his heart nearly burst. A muffled metallic clink came from underfoot. The sound wasn't loud, but it was loud enough.

A twig breaking or leaves rattling are all normal sounds of the forest. Squirrels, chipmunks, or raccoons make these kinds of sounds hundreds of times a day, and to a feeding deer, or strutting turkey, it might not even warrant a second thought. But this sound was far from normal. Nothing occurring naturally in the forest made that kind of sound. Taking a step backwards, he held the bow at the ready. Eyes and ears straining, he stood statue still, prepared to either dodge a rampaging animal or shoot if he could. Slow seconds ticked by, but nothing came, and feeling like nothing was, he kneeled, brushed away grass and leaves, and saw what he stepped on. It was the Captain's shotgun.

John gingerly worked the action — the gun was empty. Had the Captain abandoned it, before reloading, or had it been knocked from his hands? John searched the ground as far as he could see for any evidence that would help explain. He found two spent shells lying in the tall grass a few steps further into the field. He stood, and began to move forward, when the walkie-talkie in his pocket made a noise. The blank sounds of someone pressing the mic but not talking came on and off three times.

The universal sign of distress!

He covered the small speaker with his hand, and pressed the button to talk. "Hello? Hello? Detective Triplett? Is that you?"

There was a pregnant pause, and then the sound of the mic blipped again. "Yes, it's me. I just saw you kneel and fumble with something on the ground? Was that the shotgun?"

"Yes," John said, eyes up, searching for the detective.

"Are there any shells left in it?"

"No."

"Okay. Stand still and just listen for a minute. I'm in the crotch of a tree fifty yards down the field, at your ten o'clock position."

John searched the wood line, and then saw the blob of a figure perched about ten feet above the ground. Detective Triplett had both feet wedged in the split trunk of an oak tree, holding on with one hand, and waving in small motions with the other. He brought the free hand back to his face. "Do you see me?"

"Yes."

"Okay. The buck is behind me in the woods further down the field, or at least he was a few minutes ago. I haven't seen or heard him come back by, but I can't guarantee that. My Glock is somewhere between us in the grass. It slipped my grip when I was running. I think there's three, maybe four rounds left in it. Do you see where I ran through the grass?"

John looked ahead and easily recognized the disturbed trail through the field, long striding steps evidenced by the grass crushed and laid over.

"It's laying somewhere probably on the right side of the line I took when I ran. I can't see it from here. Maybe you can look for it? But before you do, go ahead and pick out a tree to climb right now. If I see him coming, I'll warn you and you can move."

"What about your backup pistol? The .38?"

"I shot that out after I climbed the tree. No service pistol is accurate at long ranges, and that snub-nose is worse than my Glock. Like an idiot, I panicked and didn't wait for him to get close enough. I may have hit him, but not good enough to stop him." The radio fell silent, then Triplett said, "I see you have your bow, but you really need to find my pistol if you can."

John spoke back into the radio. "Where's the Captain?"

"Dunno. The buck came at him first. I didn't even see him until the shotgun opened up. Jonas shot at him from the hip a couple times, but I don't think he ever connected. I saw the rounds bring up mud in front of the charge, and then he was flipping end over end behind me, the deer right on top of him. I shot a few times, but he was moving too fast. He pushed Meyers into the woods before I could catch up to him."

The grass Triplett mentioned was actually winter wheat and rye, planted as a food source for the deer to browse through the winter. It had been grazed heavily in parts of the field, but neglected where John stood. The lush vegetation was nearly shin high, and covered the ground like a thick green blanket.

That's what I get for having nice food plots.

With every deliberately slow step, his head swiveled back and forth, scanning the area. He was on his seventh step when a low moan rose from the woods across the field. It sounded again, reminding John of the painful guttural lowing of a cow in labor. John scanned the wood line to his right, saw nothing, and then turned back to Triplett, still perched in the tree. The detective waved his free hand again, then the radio said, "That's got to be Meyers. He must still be alive."

John took a couple of steps towards the sound, and saw something lying in a spot of bent-over grass. It was a single shoe. The radio came back to life. "No John. You've got to find my Glock. It's the only way you can help him now. If we can hear him, the deer can too. He might be over there right now waiting for somebody to show up. You can't risk it. Nobody will be safe until the deer is dead, and to do that, you've got to find that pistol."

Ignoring the warning, John slowly walked across the field towards the sound.

Chapter 18

Sensitive ears twitched again, scanning — sensing. The explosions at close range had hurt them earlier, but the ringing was now gone, and the buck worked them back and forth, front and back insisting on filtering out even the smallest interruptions. There was nothing for a while, only the rhythmic hops, slight as they might be, from one of those small gray rodents scavenging for the fruit of the trees. Other than that, the field was silent, the woods around them were silent, the two he attacked were silent. If a deer could smile, this one would have, knowing the reason why the one he left at the base of that tree had not stirred. He was most likely dead.

While he stood, admiring the savage goring he'd authored just minutes earlier, it came to him. The sound was so faint, he almost missed it completely, but what met his ears was a mind teasing, high pitched *click*. A heavy dose of adrenaline suddenly rushed into his veins, as he turned his head to where he thought the sound came from, and nervously flicked that magnificent white tail. Even though it came from the other side of the field, it was not a sound of the forest. Nothing that clicked ever came from the woods. He had heard the sound before, or ones like it. It was something that could be heard from the strange structure in the opening near the other end of the flowing pool, the place where he had stolen the doe's body.

Fighting the urge to bolt, the animal stood still, waiting for whatever else might follow. Movement meant noise, and as slight as the sound was, he needed complete silence if he was going to track it. A presence was nearby, that was certain, but he needed more to help him determine exactly what was walking on his web.

Ears twitching, the strange murmurings started again. It was coming from the one who had climbed and another, presumably standing where the first two had entered the opening. Without good eyes to see, a sense of dread began to build, but even the deer understood that the new presence was alone. Somewhere within his primitive brain, two more notions manifested. Where do they all come from? And after this one, how many more would be sent?

Hunger disrupted primitive thoughts, as hollow pains ran rampant through his long and lean body. The desire to feed was overwhelming, but the animal couldn't make himself go into the open. The sweet, yellow kernels were still there, he could still smell it, but first he had to deal with another one. With everything it felt, there also was a slight sense of ease. Every one of them so far was fragile; all of them cried and leaked red easily. He would make this new one pour red too.

The animal looked right, but hesitated. He wanted the place that worked so well before, but the one that climbed was between him and it. Instead, he moved left through the dampness, keeping the opening in sight. The understory was sparse; that was good for now — allowing him to move with minimal sound. The openness would not always be an ally though. Whatever those things were suffered from poor sensory, but when it was time to attack, it would not be a surprise. He would surely be seen.

The situation was becoming more desperate with each passing second. If the strange film was not affecting his sight, hunger itself might have blinded him. He weaved through the timber in a low crouch, trying to make himself as small as possible. It seemed to work. The one in the tree was still gesturing and murmuring, and seemingly hadn't spotted the movement.

The buck was almost at a run, when the legs beneath him began to tingle and lose feeling. At the same time, the long brown needles and leaves lying on the ground started building into an unbelievable heat. The lost sensitivity was somehow being transferred solely to the animal's hooves, and if the sensation kept building, in just moments, the ability to just stand would be nearly impossible. The animal did not understand what was going on, or why it was happening, he just knew that nothing felt right anymore. He was falling apart, and it all stemmed somehow from the sensations he was feeling — heat against his tender hooves, and the hunger in his belly. He needed the yellow stuff again. That always made him feel better.

The incessant murmurings continued from the field, and all at once the irritation concentrated itself in the middle of his brain. As clearly as he had ever understood anything before, basic feelings of thirst, hunger, fear, or contentment, he now understood what needed to be done. Whatever the cost, this new threat had to be neutralized.

He was within a hundred yards of where he finished attacking the first one when a new sound registered. It was a long, drawn out, pitiful, lonely, mournful sound of something close to death. He had heard it before from the striped tailed critters along the long openings where the things with glowing eyes rolled on black circles. Yet he knew that wasn't it. The sound itself was not familiar; any animal suffering from pain could make it. No, it was the tone and frequency that he recognized. There was no way to know exactly what the new sound communicated between the strange ones meant, but at least he did know what was making it. Perhaps it was a distress call? They did seem to move around in small packs; maybe it was a call to the new one for help? If that was the case, he would find a way to end it there.

Hooves continued to burn while those acute ears pinpointed the sound, and moving with no regard to the wind, the animal boldly advanced. He came to a downed oak; the destroyed canopy scattered across the ground still held a few leaves hanging from broken intertwining branches. He maneuvered himself into a small alcove along its periphery. The new hiding place provided just enough cover to break up his outline, as his brown coat blended well with the rotting branches and leaves around him.

There he waited for his chance. Hooves burning ever hotter, he shifted weight back and forth lifting one leg at a time trying to ease the building pain. While he danced, the buck considered the distance. Through the fog, afflicted eyes could barely see movement from the one on the ground. Six or seven good bounds would get him there from the cover; a little too far for his liking, but there was nothing else between them but tree trunks. It would have to do. Maybe it would be all he needed.

Chapter 19

John found him sitting at the base of a hollowed out tree. The Captain was conscious, though just barely, and he looked like he had waded through the same hell Al, Renn, and Kirby had suffered . . . only Meyers had somehow lived. His face was badly cut, gouged, and bruised, and his left eye bulged from its socket, dangling grotesquely from muscle and nerves over a badly swollen cheek. John was not sure if it would ever work again. Meyers' right shoulder sagged noticeably, and the useless hand hanging at the end of that arm donned bloody, splayed fingers that seemed to point in every direction. John was sure that shaking hands with the Captain now, would feel like grabbing a bag of loose change.

Avoiding his face and shoulder, he quickly patted him down performing a type of crude triage. A thought quickly came to him, and he asked the question to the semi-conscious Captain, "How are you still alive? Those tines should have riddled you."

Unzipping Meyers' jacket, John saw no holes or blood stains on the shirt beneath. He carefully lifted it and saw plenty of bruising, and probably what were two or three broken ribs, but there were no deadly puncture wounds like the others had. He inspected the rest of him, and found nothing of any life-threatening concern, but there was something almost comical about his feet. The Captain was wearing only one shoe; his left foot pointed skyward covered only with a navy blue sock. The one he found in the field matched the one still tied on his right foot perfectly. John shook his head. The buck hit him hard, all right — hard enough to knock him clear out of his shoes.

Captain Meyers was indeed a lucky man. The broken bones, gouges, and that freakish eye all needed attention, but against all odds he was alive. John kneeled in front of him trying to decide whether or not he needed to push that eye back in its socket, when another thought came to him. He said in a whisper, a reply to the Captain's low moans, "You and Donnie both missed the antler tines. How is that possible?"

Then he remembered what Butters had said on the radio. 'They pulled what looked like a twelve-inch deer antler out of the radiator.' John wiped a trickle of blood from Meyers' upper lip and said, "That maniac buck must have broken more than that one off sparring with trucks, and tractors, or whatever else he could find to fight."

The kid stood, took a couple of steps back and surveyed the scene. It didn't take a double dose of imagination to see what had happened. The initial impact back in the field must have been savage; forceful enough to knock him completely out of his shoe, into the air backwards, end over end. The animal was then quickly on him, pushing, driving, goring, forcing him into the woods before a frantic Triplett, who had been shocked into temporary paralysis, could react, wasting ammo; shooting at everything and anything, but hitting nothing. John had followed the furrow plowed through the leaves from the field, passing by numerous smaller trees. He supposed that they were not big enough to do the job. Amazingly, the disturbance along the ground lead directly to the largest tree in sight — a massive longleaf pine with a life-saving large hollow at the base of the trunk.

Meyers sat there now, slumped in the recess of the cavity, blood still dripping from his crooked nose. It looked as if he had been there for decades, and the tree was slowly trying to grow itself shut around him. A few feet above the ground, both edges of the hollow were scarred, and bare white wood glimmered through the shredded bark. His eye caught a smear of red against the splintered white sapwood just above Meyers' crushed hand. Closer inspection revealed way more than just that smear. Leaning, he saw a large splatter of blood on that side of the tree. John looked at the broken and bloody hand again, slowly piecing together the puzzle. Meyers must have been conscious and fighting, probably grabbing at the antlers, trying to cushion the blows. It was obvious that the Captain was slammed into the tree trunk, but something stopped the charge.

That's it! The antler's main beams must have hit both sides of the hollow. That's why bare wood is showing. That must have stopped him, and the Captain's hand must have gotten caught between the tree and the antler when it hit.

John read the clues like an expert detective. The buck's intent seemed to be to slam Meyers into the base of that pine tree until he was dead, like he had done to Al, but the hollow had not registered. Head lowered and pushing, the animal's antlers had impacted the leading edges of the concavity before Meyers hit the backside of it. With no tines to impale, he simply bounced around harmlessly in the shallow void, while the animal fruitlessly lunged against the big pine — the Captain's right hand catching the worst of it. Antler tines or not, it was clear that he should have died right there. What happened that morning, and where Meyers ended up was nothing short of divine providence.

Still reeling over what apparently happened, John began to realize that helping the Captain was going to be impossible. One person was not going to get him out of the woods. It was too far to carry him, and such an attempt would likely inflict more damage, especially around those shattered ribs. He needed Triplett.

John was quickly back on the walkie talkie, but before the detective could respond, he heard what sounded like a rush of wind coming at him, and for the briefest of moments, he thought he could smell lemons. John turned in time to glimpse a streak of brown charging at full bore. Actually thinking about what to do would have been futile, and in that split-second, there was only time to react. Before the small radio hit the ground, the bow was up and the arrow flew.

What happened next all seemed to elapse in slow motion. John, like watching the scene unfold from outside of his body, saw the wooden shaft and white feather fletching leave the bow and screw through the air towards the animal. He could tell right away that it wasn't going to be a perfect shot. The arrow was flying a touch high and right of center, but even a little off like that, it was still going to produce a devastating wound. The arrow was halfway there when the animal reacted. Those incredible senses engaged, and subsequent lightning-fast reflexes managed a hard dip, and the buck nearly dodged the arrow completely — but not quite. At just ten feet from John, the arrow sank to the fletching in the animal's left shoulder, the razor-sharp broadhead cutting a channel through tissue and bone, and coming to rest against a rear rib. The beast's front end buckled, but those black maniac eyes still fixed on the target seemed to will it on. Back hooves churning, the falling animal lurched forward with killing intensity. John took the charge, plowed over by two hundred pounds of angry venison.

He was completely out for a few seconds, and when he opened his eyes, all he could see was the deer's white belly above him, blood splattering, and four feet stomping sharp hooves into whatever they could. The first impulse was to roll, and he tucked into a ball and tried moving to the left and then to the right, but there was no escape. Those crazy pounding legs blocked his every move. John tried to cover his head, as hooves came down again and again on his chest and midsection, snapping a lower rib, and opening three jagged holes on his side. John screamed a curse, feeling his own hot, slick fluids pouring down his side just before being jolted by a cutting, electric pulse of pain.

The animal was relentless, but the arrow was starting to take a toll. The stomping began to slow, and fatigued, the buck changed attack strategies. A powerful head came down, and there was sudden and intense pressure on John's sternum. Sliding along the ground under the massive force, he frantically grabbed at head and antlers, desperately trying to fight back. He could see the jagged lumps along the main antler beam where those unbelievably long tines once turned upward, but now were completely gone. John's suspicions of why Meyers and Donnie had lived was right.

It was all a frantic brown blur, but at some point, John could clearly see a furry ear flash across his face. He craned his neck and bit down hard, tearing off a mouthful of hair, skin, and cartilage. Bellowing in pain, the animal rose off him momentarily, and that's when John's quick eyes finally saw it. There, sticking out of the buck's shoulder was his arrow's white fletching. Finally, the animal had given him a chance.

He groped. He strained. And just before he thought consciousness would slip away, the shaft was firmly in his right hand. With every last ounce of strength John pulled. The arrow backed out of the wound a foot before the wide broadhead stopped against the shoulder bone, and the crazed animal shuttered and screamed. John somehow managed a smile.

I'm not done yet, Bucky-boy. Now it's my turn to turn the screws on you.

Taking a firmer grip, he adjusted the angle as much as he could without breaking the shaft, and rammed the arrow home again. The arrow plunged deeply into the soft tissue, driving the sharp piece of metal between two of the forward ribs, and into the chest cavity. As lucky as John was gaining the arrow, there would be no second attempt. The buck emanated another blood chilling scream, and staggered backwards, breaking the end of the arrow off in John's hand.

Blinking those dead black eyes, frothy mucus forming at the buck's nostrils began to turn red. John's primitive riposte thrust had managed to find some part of the lungs, but there was no time to take a breath, as those hellish hooves began to piston again. John squirmed trying to break free, and his bow that had been lying in the leaves by him the whole time rubbed against his arm. He knew what it was immediately, and he maneuvered under the beast enough to pick it up. Now all he needed was an arrow. His free hand went over his shoulder, probing for the back quiver, but it was no use. The buck countered his every move, and John, lying on the ground still eating hooves, simply could not reach them.

He was starting to lose hope when a shot exploded at close range. There was a dull thud above him — the sound of bullet hitting flesh — and a hot splash of blood hit him in the face. Another explosion ripped the still air, and instantly one of the buck's remaining antler beams splintered. Two more shots quickly came in succession, but didn't seem to hit anything. John turned his head and saw Detective Triplett standing there holding the Glock. A stream of smoke trickled from the end of the barrel, and the slide was locked back. At scarcely ten steps, only two of the four shots had connected.

How could he have missed from that close?

There was no time to ponder the answers, and before John could blink, the wounded buck was charging. Triplett stood unbelieving, frozen in fear, arms extended, still aiming the useless pistol. And then the buck hit him.

John tried to get to his knees. His side burned, and the ring finger on his left hand felt either broken or badly dislocated. His ears rang loudly from the explosions, but he still managed to hear Triplett's screams. John felt the bow in his hand and instinctively reached for arrows. The first one was in his hand and on the string before he realized the shaft was broken inches behind where the broadhead should have been. Quickly he threw it aside and pulled another. Broken. Another — broken. Another — this one wasn't broken, but was badly cracked. The next one he pulled was in one piece and straight.

The buck was facing away from him, his two massive haunches working legs of torture. John wanted to move to the side, where he could get an easy shot through both lungs while the animal was focused on killing the detective. But when he tried to stand, he thought he felt something sliding out of one of the big holes in his side. Whether some or all of his guts were falling out or not, the pain was paralyzing.

Head spinning, he managed to stay on his knees, and holding the bow ready, John yelled at the buck. There was no response. He yelled again, and still there was nothing but Triplett's cries and the dull thudding of pounding hooves. John pulled his last arrow, intact and straight, and he carefully laid it on the ground beside him. He spit a mouthful of blood, and said with a growl through gritted teeth, "I wonder how you'd like a sharp broadhead shot right up your ass?"

He steadied himself, took a deep breath, and tried to draw the bow. The bowstring came back slowly, while the holes in his side poured blood and ached. The string stopped well before his normal anchoring position, and he let it back down. Drawing the bow seemed impossible — the pain was too much. He shook his head, trying to clear his mind. If he couldn't shoot the bow, there was a very good chance Detective Jefferson Triplett would die.

John set his jaw, and hauled back on the bow again. The arrow shaft slid across his fist at the bow's handle, and suddenly his right hand, holding the bowstring, came to that familiar spot on his cheek. He held the draw for a moment, and while trying to forget the pain, he focused on the buck's dark anus, surrounded by a cloud of gleaming white fur.

Concentrate . . . Concentrate . . . Concentrate . . .

When the green light went on, the string slipped from his fingers, leaving just a blur of white feather fletching. John's eyes followed it, and his heart sank. The arrow was well below his focus, and looked as if it might miss the animal completely. But down below the buck's rear port hung yet another sensitive target, one that would serve the purpose equally as well. Thunderstruck, the teen watched sharp twisting blades spin into the animal's scrotum, just before disappearing completely low in its paunch — a kind of crude, but instant castration.

At first, John didn't believe what he saw. The arrow was there one second and gone the next. He actually thought for an instant that he had missed, but the animal's reaction confirmed what John's eyes beheld. Another shriek of pain came from the buck's bloody throat just before he convulsed into something that looked like a bucking bronco trying to throw a cowboy. A clear stream of dark blood mixed with corn, and other green chunks of undigested matter erupted from the wound. The buck lunged forward off Triplett, and spun, facing John. He stumbled and swayed, but managed to keep his feet under him. The massive animal lowered his head, preparing to charge again.

Okay Johnny-boy, now you've done it. You've got his attention. Nuts and guts won't kill him right away, but maybe it will slow him down just a little. He's gonna come again but this time, it ends.

The prediction was true. The bleeding animal straightened, found its target, and lunged. John, still on his knees, grabbed for the other arrow. "I've got something else for you right here you son of a bitch."

Twenty yards.

Fifteen yards.

Ten yards.

The wild locomotive was building speed, and over the drawn arrow, John could see bloody mucous spewing from his nose, ears laid back, those terrible black eyes, and yellow teeth gleaming. The charge was with everything the buck had left. Win or lose, this was it.

The shot was true the instant it left the bow, and for a split second, all he could see was that practice arrow disappearing into that armadillo's head back in the camp yard. John blinked away the past just in time for the present, and watched nearly in awe as his arrow broke teeth and rammed itself squarely into the charging beast's mouth. The massive animal buckled, but the momentum from the charge still prevailed. John, like detective Triplett, stood there frozen, unbelieving.

Chapter 20

John couldn't remember much about it. It was as if some supernatural force interceded at the very moment of impact, completely erasing his memory of the pain and shock. The crazed deer charged, and hit him, but everything after that was just a blur. There were only two things he felt sure of. He felt the bow slip from his hand while he was tumbling backwards, head over heels, as a kid might be tossed in the surf at the beach, and sometime in the melee, he felt the cold panic of having the breath knocked out of him.

He came back to himself lying face down in the leaves, gasping for air. He struggled to turn his head to the side, and the buck was lying next to him, heaving, convulsing, bleeding, then it was over. John smiled just for a moment, but then the pain was back, intense and overwhelming, and before he could do anything, blackness overcame him again . . . and then there was nothing.

For a while, it all felt like a weird, anecdotal dream. He tried to open his eyes, but it was like being in a dark cellar, pushing upward against unmovable doors that were blocking the light of day. Even in his semi-consciousness, he understood that the deer was dead, but there was still a sense of dread looming. Was he alive? Was he dead, or dying? He couldn't really tell. Sounds and what he thought were voices came to him, but he couldn't make sense of them. Whatever it was seemed to be a jumbled and garbled form of double-talk and unintelligent screeching.

The sounds came and went, and after what could have been two minutes or two days, John, channeling all of his focus and energy, managed to open his eyes. At first there was nothing but multi-colored blurs floating around in that creamy fog, but finally, his vision cleared enough to see what he thought were trees and clouds oddly dancing above him. The voices were gone now, but everything seemed to be moving in rhythm with the sounds of labored breathing, and a strange crunching sound from below. His mind could only think of soldiers marching in unison across popped popcorn.

The trees and clouds began to blur, as he felt unconsciousness sneaking up on him. He tried to hold on, but those fuzzy blobs started swirling together above him like flowing lava. He felt sick to his stomach, and he closed his eyes, trying not to throw up. Then as if someone flipped a switch, he saw, heard, and felt nothing, except the strange sensation of being cold.

***

When John finally came to, he was lying on a spine board, wind whipped by a helicopter's working rotors. The prop wash made his eyes water and the cuts on his face sting. Down by his elbow, his side still screamed with electric pulses of pain. He could hear people moving around him, but he couldn't turn his head to see who they were. Facing up, there was nothing but an endless gray sky through the blurred circle of rotors. His lips were dry, his throat burned, but he took the pain and tried to speak. "Hey? Hey! Who's there? Dad? Somebody?"

Sheriff Butters appeared over him, wearing that same easy smile. The ends of his handlebar mustache lightly fluttered in the turbulence. He yelled, trying to overcome the blaring sound of the helicopter. "Well, well, now. Good to have you back with us, young man."

John eye's flashed wildly back and forth, trying to make sense of it all. He tried to raise his head again, but it wouldn't move. He could feel something pressing against his neck and chin, and realized that he was wearing one of those wide whiplash collars around his neck. If he could have looked down on himself, he would have also seen the head support halo and the heavy strap across it just above his forehead. Two more identical straps crossed him securing the rest of his body to the board: one at mid-body and the other at his knees.

Butters said, "Just lay still, John. They have you strapped down and ready to go. I know you're scared, son, and things probably don't make too much sense, but don't worry." He looked down and made a circular gesture with his fingers at the neck brace, "They say all this is just precautionary, just in case you have some kind of neck or head injury." The Sheriff smiled and gently adjusted the strap across John's chest. "It'll also keep you from standing up and walking right out of the bird on the way to Montgomery, if you happen to go out again and come to, confused as to where you are and what's going on. You know what they say about an ounce of prevention don't you?"

John understood, and tried to nod. "What happened? Where are Meyers and Triplett?"

The Sheriff cut an eye to the left and motioned with his thumb. "They are right beside you, all done up the same way. How in the world y'all managed to wind up on the same flight is beyond me. Bound to have used the same travel agent — probably going to have to spend a little time at the same hotel too."

John was trying to process the joke, when Butters' face changed. The easy going smile vanished, replaced by an almost expressionless glare. He grabbed John's open collar, curling it into his fist, and nose to nose, he said in an almost scary voice, "You know you scared the hell out of me with that John Wayne crap you pulled back there . . . right?"

Confused, John blinked several times, wondering if he had heard the Sheriff correctly.

"I need you to understand one thing, John. The next time I give you a direct order, whether you work for me or not, I expect you to follow it. You understand? Heroes get to live only on television; in real life they die."

The sternness seemed to melt away as quickly as it had come, and the Sheriff smiled and released and straightened John's collar. "But I'm glad that you didn't listen to me this time. You nearly did yourself in," the Sheriff chinned to the left, "but I'll believe to my dying day that you saved their lives."

John managed to relax a little. "They okay?"

"Oh yeah, sure. Triplett has a broken arm, cuts and scrapes, and a busted tooth or two. He's in pretty good shape, considering, but it looks like he's gonna miss that court date this morning after all."

John managed a smile, and almost laughed. It made his side hurt. "What about the Captain?"

"Jonas didn't fare quite so well. EMTs say his collar bone, and likely the ball and socket in his shoulder are busted six ways to Sunday, and that right hand of his might need some surgery before he can quick draw again.

Both are going to need plenty of stitches here and there, but nothing that's going to force either into early retirement."

"What about his eye?"

"Well, they don't know about that yet. Gonna let the Big Dollars have a look at it when they get y'all to Montgomery. Terrible thing to look at though. They put a big patch over it and have half of his head wrapped so he won't scare the women and children between here and the hospital."

John winced against a new wave of pain attacking his side. He bit his lip and forced his eyes open. "Would you do me a favor?"

"Sure kid, anything."

John took a deep breath and wetted his lips with the tip of his tongue. "When you get back, call my folks and tell them — tell them what happened, and that I'm okay. Oh, and you might want to tell dad he owes me for an armadillo I killed at hunting camp."

The Sheriff laughed out loud. "I think you're going to pull through after all. And you know something else? Now that you mention it, I believe Miss Judy said something about that on the way down. Clay called the office while we were getting Donnie squared away. Something about the airport up there was open and they were going to charter a flight back. One of those fast twin-engine jobs. I believe she said they were taking off around eight." Butters pushed up his sleeve, and looked at his watch, figuring. "Chartered plane — direct flight from St. Louis — hmmm. They're liable to beat you back to Montgomery."

The Sheriff lightly patted John on the shoulder. "Don't worry. When y'all take off, I'm gonna get her to call the airport and make the arrangements. I'll guarantee that you'll see your ma and pa sometime today."

John felt something cold and wet on his arm, then a small sting. The Sheriff nodded at whoever was there, and turned back, smiling again. "Just a little something for the pain. You'll be right as rain in just a minute or two."

John could already feel it working as a wave of warmness came over him. The fire in his side eased, and his lips and fingertips tingled in a funny way. The Sheriff was talking again, but John didn't care. Something about being proud, and if he ever decided to hang up his typewriter for police work, he would give him one helluva recommendation anywhere.

Butters' lips were still moving, but his voice trailed off, meshing evenly into the dull hum of the rotors. John was drifting on a cloud of his own haze when he felt what he thought was somebody tapping him on the leg. The spine board he was strapped to magically levitated and moved into the large open area behind the helicopter's cockpit. Over the staggering noise that now oddly sounded like music, he heard a voice say in radio talk that they were airborne and leaving Halifax headed to Montgomery. Feeling no pain, John's smile widened. It was the best news he'd heard all week.

CPSIA information can be obtained
at www.ICGtesting.com
Printed in the USA
BVOW09s1351290517
485397BV00001B/20/P